'I don't want against my wi she said, 'I can't understand what you're hoping to gain, why you went to so much trouble to get me here.'

He took a stray tendril of blonde hair that had escaped and tugged it gently, making her flinch away. 'It was no trouble. In fact the whole thing worked incredibly smoothly.'

She gritted her teeth. 'Why——?'

'We'll talk about it after dinner.'

'I don't want any dinner.'

His green lazy-river eyes heavy-lidded and sensual, he said, 'Well, if you really don't want to eat, I can think of something a great deal more exciting to do…'

Wondering frantically if he meant what she thought he meant, she stared up at him.

Softly, he went on, 'So it will suit me fine if you decide against eating.' He held out both hands. 'Shall we go upstairs?'

Lee Wilkinson lives with her husband in a three-hundred-year-old stone cottage in a Derbyshire village, which most winters gets cut off by snow. They both enjoy travelling and recently, joining forces with their daughter and son-in-law, spent a year going round the world 'on a shoestring' while their son looked after Kelly, their much loved German shepherd dog. Her hobbies are reading and gardening, and holding impromptu barbecues for her long-suffering family and friends.

Recent titles by the same author:

ONE NIGHT WITH THE TYCOON
HIS MISTRESS BY MARRIAGE
THE CARLOTTA DIAMOND

KEPT BY THE TYCOON

BY
LEE WILKINSON

MILLS & BOON®

First published in Great Britain 2006
Harlequin Mills & Boon Limited,
Eton House, 18-24 Paradise Road, Richmond, Surrey TW9 1SR

© Lee Wilkinson 2006

ISBN 0 263 84823 X

Set in Times Roman 10½ on 11½ pt.
01-0606-51905

Printed and bound in Spain
by Litografia Rosés, S.A., Barcelona

CHAPTER ONE

THE physiotherapy room at Mayfair's exclusive Grizedale Clinic was quiet and peaceful, the only sound the muted background roar of London's traffic. A deep-pile carpet covered the floor, a vase of crimson roses scented the air and a black leather couch was spread with a spotless sheet ready for its next occupant.

At the open window muslin curtains lifted in the slight breeze, allowing light to enter but keeping the lingering summer-in-the-city heat at bay.

Wearing a silky, charcoal-grey suit and an ivory blouse, her long, naturally blonde hair taken up in a coil, Madeleine was sitting at the desk, updating her previous patient's file, when there was a tap, and the door opened.

Neat in her blue uniform, dark curls secured in the nape of her neck by a gilt clip, Eve came in with some notes.

Eve Collins, along with her brother Noel, had been Madeleine's friend since their nursery-school days.

It had been Eve who had mentioned this post at the clinic. 'If you're interested, Maddy, the woman who usually fills it has taken maternity leave, which means it will only be temporary.

'But I promise you the surroundings are pleasant, and the money's good, so this might be just what you need to tide you over until you've built up a clientele of patients...

'That is, if you don't mind working four evenings a week throughout the summer months…'

'I don't mind at all,' Madeleine had said gratefully, 'and I'd be glad of both the money and the experience.'

'I'll mention your name to Mrs Bond, who deals with personnel.'

On being offered the post, Madeleine had started work immediately. It meant she could no longer see her mother in the evenings, but she had reorganised her daytime routine to fit in visits to the nursing home between her private patients.

Smiling at her friend, Eve put the notes she was carrying on the desk and, her blue eyes gleaming with excitement, hurried into speech. 'Your last patient for tonight is a new one, a Rafe Lombard…'

Then dropping her voice to a whisper, 'And boy, is he *gorgeous*! A real hunk, with all the charm of a young Sasha Distel! Tall, dark and handsome may be an overworked phrase, but there's no other way to describe him.'

Madeleine sighed and raised her eyes to heaven. 'The last time you told me someone was gorgeous he turned out to have pimples and dandruff.'

'Scoff if you must, but this time you'll have to admit I'm not exaggerating. All the female staff are in a tizzy, married and single alike.

'When he smiled at Thelma, who you must admit is a bit of a man-hater, she went weak at the knees and dropped all the papers she was carrying.'

'Well, you'd better send this gorgeous hunk in,' Madeleine said drily. 'Otherwise I won't have time to take a look at him.'

A moment or so later the latch clicked, and, pushing aside the notes she had just scanned through, Madeleine glanced up.

The man who entered the room carried with him an air of power, of self-reliance and quiet authority.

As she looked at this ruggedly handsome, perfect stranger, everything stopped—her breathing, her heart, the blood in her veins...even the world ceased to spin on its axis.

It was as if she'd always known him. As if she had just been marking time, waiting for him to appear. Waiting for him to fill the void she had been only too aware of, even while she was married to Colin.

Rather than rushing into speech, as many of her patients did, he stood quite still, his forest-green eyes fixed on her face.

Dragging air into her lungs, she struggled to pull herself together. Though it seemed an eternity, it could only have been a few seconds before she succeeded in regaining at least some outward semblance of composure.

His effect on her had been pure and immediate and total, and she knew instinctively that she must stay cool and aloof, or be lost.

For perhaps the first time she understood fully why every tutor on the physiotherapy courses—apart from Colin—had found it necessary to warn their pupils not to allow themselves to get emotionally involved with any of their patients.

And, when it came to the crunch, how useless that warning was.

Drawing another deep, steadying breath, she rose to her feet and, daring her knees to tremble, advanced to meet him, holding out her hand. 'Mr Lombard, I'm Madeleine Knight...'

He took her hand in a firm grip and smiled, he looked deep into her eyes and nearly stopped her heart for a second time.

Her breathing impeded, her throat desert dry, she began, 'I understand you've suffered a possible whiplash injury. When did it happen?'

'Earlier this evening.'

His voice, low-pitched and slightly husky, shivered along her nerve ends.

Those clear green eyes lingering on her face, he added, 'Since then I've had some discomfort. I don't think it's anything to worry about, but I was advised to see a physiotherapist just in case there was any muscle damage.'

In spite of all her efforts her voice wasn't quite steady as she asked, 'How did it happen?'

'I was taking my racing car round a private circuit when the steering went.' Drily, he added, 'Straw bales can seem remarkably solid at speed.'

He was still watching her and that steady appraisal threw her far more than any of her previous male patients' attempts at flirtation.

'If you could strip to the waist and get up on the couch so I can check it out, please?' She tried to sound cool and professional, in control.

While Madeleine kept her eyes fixed firmly on his notes he took off his jacket and shirt and draped them over a chair, before hitching himself up to sit on the couch.

Only when he was settled did she look up.

His back was straight and muscular, the line of his spine elegant, as the broad shoulders tapered to a lean waist and narrow hips. His clear, tanned skin carried the glow of health and gleamed like oiled silk, making her want to touch it.

Even the back of his well-shaped head was attractive and sexy, the short dark hair curling a little into the nape of his neck.

Taking a deep breath, she went over to him and, concentrating fiercely on her professional task, with firm but gentle hands began her examination.

Though he must have been well aware of his effect on women, he made no suggestive remarks, nor did he try to chat her up. Instead he sat quietly, obediently raising his arms and flexing his muscles when asked to.

As soon as she had finished the examination, she said briskly, 'Right, Mr Lombard…' and moved away to a safer distance.

As he swung his feet to the floor she confirmed, 'Though there's some obvious stiffness in the neck and shoulder muscles, luckily there's no evidence of any real damage. In a few days, if all goes well, you should be back to normal.'

'That's great.' He smiled at her, his smile a white slash across his tanned face.

She watched as his lean cheeks creased, and a fan of fine laughter lines appeared at the corners of those fascinating almond-shaped eyes. Eyes that tilted up at the outer corners. Eyes that would have made even the most ordinary face appear extraordinary. And his face was far from ordinary...

Dragging her gaze away with an effort, and trying to ignore the way his smile had sent her pulses racing madly, she went on, 'Rest is all it needs until after the weekend. Then I suggest you have a further check just to be on the safe side.'

Looking directly into the clear aquamarine eyes of this cool, fascinating woman, who seemed totally unaware of her own beauty, he asked, 'So when shall I see you again?'

His intent gaze and the question, phrased as it was, shook her rigid.

But seeing him again, even in a professional capacity, would be far too dangerous. It would be courting disaster.

The clinic's policy was that a strict protocol should be observed between staff and clients, and, faced with soaring costs at the nursing home, she couldn't afford to lose this job.

'Perhaps you'd like to come in again on Monday or Tuesday morning?'

He shook his head. 'Evening would suit me better.'

Biting her bottom lip, she made a pretence of studying her appointments before she suggested evenly, 'In that case, suppose you make it Monday evening at the same time?'

Mrs Deering, the plump, middle-aged and happily married part-timer who worked weekends and Monday evenings, could hopefully help him without any threat to her peace of mind or her position.

'That suits me fine.'

'Then I'll say goodnight, Mr Lombard.'

'*Au revoir*, Miss Knight. Many thanks.' He strode to the door and made his way out.

Some element of vitality went with him, and she was left feeling, *life goes that way*.

With a hollow emptiness in the pit of her stomach she sank down at her desk and, with the image of his dark, attractive face filling her mind, started to update his notes.

The notes finished, she was sitting there gazing into space when the door opened and Eve came back in. 'I wondered if you were still here… Almost everyone else has gone.'

With nothing to look forward to but a solitary supper, there had been no incentive for Madeleine to hurry home.

'So what did you think of Rafe Lombard?'

'He was every bit as gorgeous as you said,' Madeleine answered as lightly as possible.

Eve looked gratified. 'And there's more…'

'More?'

'According to Joanne, who always seems to know these things, he inherited Charn Industries from Christopher Charn, his godfather… Which must make him a multimillionaire, and a prime catch.

'Though so far apparently he's managed to elude the hook and stay a bachelor. Which is a challenge in itself. A challenge I wouldn't mind taking up if I got half a chance. After all, a multimillionaire must be worth the risk of getting fired.

'Ah, well,' Eve sighed as she continued, 'I suppose I mustn't let myself dream. He's hardly likely to be interested in the likes of me. With those kinds of looks and that amount of charisma, Rafe Lombard must have women queuing up to throw themselves at his feet.'

No doubt Eve was right, Madeleine sighed, and pushed all thoughts of Rafe Lombard firmly to the back of her mind.

'Finished with these?' At the other girl's nod, Eve gathered up the notes and headed for the door. 'Well, I'm off. I've a date with Dave. See you Tuesday. Don't spend all weekend at the nursing home. Try to get out a bit.'

'I'll try.'

Since her mother had suffered severe head injuries in the gas explosion that had wrecked their rented house, she had spent most of her free time by the sick woman's bedside.

Sitting hour after hour with the corpse-like figure, talking or reading to her, not knowing how much, if anything, her mother understood, had taken a heavy toll on Madeleine.

As had the death of Madeleine's husband, Colin, in the same tragic accident. An accident she could only blame herself for.

As the weeks turned into months, finding she was no longer any fun, most of her friends had drifted away, and only Eve and Noel had stuck by her wholeheartedly.

Eve, in her usual cheerful, down-to-earth way, had provided an emotional crutch, while Noel had been there for her in a practical capacity.

First he had helped her find somewhere to live, then he had taken her out, chivvied her to eat and done his utmost to raise her spirits while she tried to pick up the pieces of her shattered life.

As a shoulder to cry on, Noel was the first to admit that he was useless. But when she had needed someone to make her laugh, to forget for a short time at least that she needed a shoulder to cry on, he had been ideal.

When he'd gone to work abroad, troubleshooting for an oil company, she had missed him. Missed his unstinting support, his irreverent tongue, his spiky sense of humour and laid-back attitude.

Missed having a man in her life.

Since she had been on her own several men had tried to get on more than friendly terms with her. But, well aware that, in the circumstances, the odds were stacked against any new relationship succeeding, she had steered clear.

After being alone so long it was time to move on, she knew, yet no one had attracted her enough to act as the catalyst to make her *want* to take the chance.

Until today. And that attraction, fierce though it was, was futile.

Becoming aware that time was slipping past, she closed the window and collected her shoulder-bag before letting herself out through a side-door and heading for the main gates.

On rainy days she caught the bus back to her Knightsbridge flat, but during the dry, settled spell of weather that had lasted for almost a week now, she had enjoyed walking home.

Tonight, however, having reached the imposing gates and turned west along Grizedale Street, she felt oddly weary and dispirited, in no mood for the thirty-minute walk.

She had just drawn level with a midnight-blue limousine that was parked by the kerb, when its rear door opened and a tall, dark-haired figure climbed out.

Dazzled by the low evening sun, she took a moment to realise that the man blocking her way was Rafe Lombard.

Surprise stopped her in her tracks, and as she shielded her eyes to look up at him he said easily, 'I thought if I hung around a while I might catch you. Have dinner with me?'

He was tall, dwarfing her with his height. If they were standing closer her head would rest on his broad chest.

Confused by the thought, she found herself stammering, 'N-no, thank you.'

'Perhaps it was stupid to spring it on you like this, but now I've admitted I'm an idiot,' he laughed, 'won't you reconsider and go out with me?'

With a flash of humour, she said, 'What? Go out with a self-confessed idiot?'

He gave her an appreciative grin. 'Think of the entertainment value.'

She shook her head. 'I can bear to give it up.'

'Surely not!' he mocked gently.

'Afraid so.'

'Go on. I promise I don't bite.'

Madeleine lowered her eyes. 'I'm sorry, but I can't.'

Putting his head on one side, he asked, 'Why not?'

His face was so full of charm that it took her breath away and turned her very bones to water.

Her voice sounding impeded, she said, 'It's against the clinic's policy for staff and clients to get familiar or meet on a social basis.'

He grimaced at the prim phrasing. 'If we do get familiar I promise not to breathe a word to a soul.'

'I'm not dressed for eating out.'

'You look absolutely fine to me.' He grinned.

Before she could make any further protest, she found herself drawn towards the car and urged into the back seat.

He slid in beside her, and she went hot all over when his muscular thigh pressed against hers as he reached to fasten first her seat belt and then his own.

Sensing that heated confusion, and warning himself not to rush things, he moved away to leave a little space between them.

With a silent sigh of relief, she glanced at him.

He met her gaze directly. The sun slanting in showed that her long-lashed aquamarine eyes had in their depths a sprinkle of gold dust, and her flawless skin a peach-like down.

His fingers itched to stroke it.

Controlling the urge, he asked lightly, 'Anywhere in particular you'd like to go?'

Wits scattered, knowing she shouldn't be here at all, she shook her head. 'No, I—'

Touching a button, he instructed the chauffeur, 'Just drive around for a while, Michael.'

As the limousine pulled smoothly away from the kerb, feeling rather as though she'd been hijacked, Madeleine began weakly, 'What made you…?'

'Chance my arm?' Rafe suggested when she hesitated. 'Sheer determination. If I'd been sure of seeing you again, I might not have rushed things. But when I made a few tactful enquiries I discovered that you wouldn't be here Monday evening…

'Which could have meant one of two things: either I was just another patient you didn't mind if you never saw again…or else someone you *could* be interested in and felt, because of the clinic's policy, you should steer clear of. I rather hoped it was the latter…'

Trying to control the surge of excitement that ran through her, she bit her lip.

Though his phrasing had been reasonably cautious, there was an air of confidence about him that suggested he felt fairly sure it *was* the latter.

And the way she had allowed herself to be shepherded into the car without protest must have reinforced that assumption.

'It opens up such possibilities…' He smiled at her. 'And I'm only too pleased you're free to explore those possibilities…'

The sexual chemistry between them was like an electrical force she could sense through every pore in her skin.

But recalling what Eve had said about women throwing themselves at his feet, and disinclined to let him believe that she might be one of them, she tried to appear cool and unmoved.

Judging by his face, her strategy hadn't worked.

In an effort to take the wind out of his sails she looked him in the eye and asked, 'What makes you so sure I'm free?'

Apparently unruffled, he answered, 'Well, for one thing, you're not wearing a ring—'

'That's nothing to go by these days.'

'True. That's why I waylaid your colleague.'

'Which colleague?'

'The pretty, dark-haired girl who first took my details. I happened to see her leaving the clinic and spoke to her. Eve, isn't it? I gather she's a good friend of yours.'

Without a blush, he added, 'I managed to coax quite a bit of information out of her.'

An edge to her voice, Madeleine asked, 'What kind of information?'

'I needed to know if you were married or in a steady relationship. When I asked her, she told me you'd lost your husband and been alone for quite a while now. I couldn't imagine a beautiful woman like you being on your own, but she seemed fairly sure there was no man in your life at the moment.'

When Madeleine merely looked at him, he added, 'Which means you have no commitments, no one waiting at home for you?'

'No.' As though he was willing her, she found herself unable to lie.

'Then I'd like to think that having dinner with me is *marginally* more appealing than eating alone?' he said quizzically.

When she made no immediate response, he urged, 'Please say it is, for the sake of my fragile ego.'

She smiled in spite of herself, a smile that brought her beauty to life and set those tiny gold flecks in her eyes dancing.

As he stared, entranced, she said a shade tartly, 'I have the distinct feeling that your ego is robust enough,' then, throwing caution to the winds, added, 'But yes, it is. *Marginally*.'

He laughed. 'A woman with spirit, I see... So where would you like to go?'

His mouth was beautiful, she thought, at once controlled and sensitive, the lower lip a little fuller than the upper. It was a mouth that tied knots in her stomach.

Somehow she managed, 'I really don't mind. Anywhere you choose.'

That was the first hurdle cleared, Rafe thought triumphantly as he instructed the chauffeur, 'The Xanadu, please, Michael.'

Knowing he shouldn't touch her—yet—but desperate to do so, he took her hand and, his thumb stroking across her palm, went on softly, 'I think you'll agree that it's the perfect setting for a romantic evening.'

She shivered.

Things were moving fast. Too fast.

Knowing she needed to apply the brakes, she withdrew her hand and, gathering herself, stared resolutely out of the car window.

But she was still breathing unevenly when they drove through tall ornamental gates and drew up outside the celebrated Mayfair restaurant.

Once a private house, the Xanadu was built in the style of a Spanish hacienda, and stood in its own discreetly floodlit gardens. Mature trees and shrubs provided a pleasant backdrop to smooth green lawns, and flowering shrubs climbed the stuccoed walls.

When the middle-aged chauffeur got out to open the door, Rafe told him, 'Don't bother hanging around, Michael. Get off home to the wife.'

His look grateful, the man said, 'Thank you, sir. Goodnight sir, madam…'

Rafe opened the thick smoked-glass door with an easy courtesy that she soon came to know was part of his nature.

Inside the foyer, his jacket was whisked away and they were greeted by the proprietor. 'Good evening, Mr Lombard…madam… How nice to see you. Your usual table?'

His *usual* table… Did he make a habit of bringing his women here? Madeleine wondered.

'Please, Henri.'

The *maître d'* appeared to show them through a series of archways to a secluded corner table in the stylish, white-walled restaurant.

Long windows looking onto the gardens were open wide, letting in warm evening air fragrant with the scent of roses and honeysuckle. A few bright stars were appearing, and a thin, silvery disc of moon floated in the blue sky.

As he'd said, it was the perfect setting for a romantic evening.

Watching her glance round, and instantly on her wavelength, he queried, 'Yes?'

'Yes,' she agreed with a smile.

While they sipped an aperitif she tried to concentrate on the menu, but, try as she might, she couldn't prevent herself looking at him, and whenever he wasn't watching her her eyes were drawn to his face.

He wasn't merely good-looking. With a cleft chin, a mouth that was at once ascetic and sensual, a strong nose, high cheekbones, brilliant, thickly lashed green eyes and dark, curved brows, he was intriguing, riveting.

But it was more than his looks. Much more. There was something about the man himself. Something she couldn't quite put a name to, but something that fulfilled a need in her. It felt right to be with him, as if she had always known him, as if they belonged together.

While they ate an excellent meal he kept the conversation light and general, moving from topic to topic, finding out what interested her, seeking her opinion on the subjects that did.

In spite of her *awareness* of him, the heated attraction that lay just beneath the surface, she found herself responding with an ease that, when she thought about it later, surprised her

It wasn't until they reached the coffee stage that he deliberately moved into more dangerous territory.

Needing to know, and recalling the levelness of her gaze even when she was flustered, he went for the direct approach. 'Tell me about your husband.'

Every nerve in her body tightening, she said, 'There's not much to tell.'

'What was his name?'

'Colin. Colin Formby.'

'You kept your maiden name?' he queried.

'Yes. It was what my family wanted,' she said quietly, taking a sip of her drink.

He raised an eyebrow quizzically. 'You were an only child?'

'Yes,' Madeleine answered.

Rafe paused, leaning back in his chair. 'What field was your husband in?'

'Physiotherapy.'

'When did the pair of you meet?'

'At university.' Madeleine lowered her gaze, focusing on anything but Rafe's probing gaze.

'You were students together?'

'No. I was in my final year. Colin was a tutor.'

Rafe was intrigued. 'So he was older than you?'

'Eighteen years.'

'A big gap.'

'Yes,' she said shortly. Madeleine had always thought that the age gap, big as it was, wouldn't have mattered if she had truly loved him.

Rafe could sense her growing discomfort, but having got this far, he decided to press on. 'How long were the two of you married?'

'Six months.'

'Not long.'

'No,' Madeleine almost whispered.

Rafe paused, knowing his questions were difficult for her. 'How did he die?'

'He was killed in an explosion.'

Quelling the urge to ask any further questions, Rafe commented, 'Tough.'

Madeleine raised her eyes to his. 'Yes, it was.'

There was sadness there and some other emotion Rafe couldn't put a name to. But it wasn't the utter desolation, the inconsolable grief, of someone who had lost all they held dear. Of that he was sure.

He breathed an inward sigh of relief. The absence of a man in her life had made him fear that she was still in love with her dead husband, but the vibes he was picking up convinced him he was wrong.

Which must make his chances of succeeding, a great deal easier, he thought.

Refilling her coffee-cup, he changed the subject smoothly. 'What does Madeleine Knight do in her spare time? Are you a secret television addict?'

Relaxing again, she laughed and shook her head. 'No, I much prefer a book.'

'Ah, a woman after my own heart! Have you read Matthew Colt's *Funny Business*…?'

'Oh, yes… I loved the part where Joe tries to steal his ex-wife's poodle…'

For a little while they talked about the book, laughing over the bits that had amused them the most, before Madeleine remarked, 'I read somewhere that it's going to be turned into a play.'

'So I understand. Should be worth seeing… Do you like the theatre?'

'Love it.'

'Have you had a chance to see the new West End play everyone's talking about?'

'*Beloved Impresario*?' She shook her head and, unwilling to admit she couldn't really afford to go to the theatre these days, said, 'I imagine tickets are like gold dust.'

'I'm sure I could get hold of a couple, if you'd like to see it?' he asked casually.

Her heart starting to hammer against her ribs, she bit back the urge to accept. She was being foolish in the extreme just having dinner with him. No doubt all he wanted was a brief fling.

But while many women might have jumped at the chance, that kind of thing wasn't her style.

Plus, it could cost her her job.

Her expression tight, controlled, she refused with formal politeness. 'I don't think so, thank you.'

He was having none of it. Green eyes looked into aquamarine. 'You mean you don't want to see it? Or you don't want to see it with me?'

Feeling as though she'd been set down in the middle of a minefield, she found herself wishing the evening were over. Wishing she could escape.

And he knew it.

Lifting her chin, she answered as steadily as possible, 'I don't have much spare time, so I don't want to commit myself.'

He had known from the start that getting anywhere with this woman wouldn't be easy. Now he realized that it was going to be a great deal harder than he had anticipated.

But he had wanted her on sight, wanted her with a passionate hunger that had surprised and shaken him. And no matter what it took, he vowed, he intended to have her.

But it would be a mistake to come on too strong.

With a graceful movement of his hand he conceded defeat and, his expression bland, steered the conversation into less perilous channels.

Feeling relieved, she followed his lead.

Watching her, he noted that relief and wondered why she was so wary, so reluctant to get involved.

Still, the night was young. There was time to change her mood.

His charming nature soon set her at her ease once more, and by the time they finally rose to leave she could have stayed there all night.

And he knew that too.

Watching her face, soft and dreamy now, he felt a strange tenderness mingling with satisfaction as he escorted her outside.

Moonlit air caressed her skin like velvet, and the stars were so close she felt she only had to stretch out a hand to pluck one from the sky.

The taxi Rafe had ordered was waiting for them, and his hand a warm weight in the middle of her spine, he ushered her towards it.

When they were settled in the back, he said, 'I understand from Miss Collins that you live in Knightsbridge. Where exactly?'

She gave him the address of her flat and, sliding open the glass panel, he relayed it to the driver.

As they reached the gates and joined the late-night stream of traffic, he looked deep into her eyes. His look was so intent and searching it made her heart beat faster and her breath grow short.

While she stared back at him as though mesmerised, he took her heart-shaped face between his palms and, bending his dark head, touched his mouth to hers.

His kiss, light and fleeting though it was, seemed to melt every bone in her body and filled her with an almost uncontrollable longing.

Drawing back, he said quizzically, 'There now, that's what you've been fearing all night, but it didn't hurt a bit, did it?'

When she just looked at him with big, dazed eyes, he said, 'So shall I do it again?'

Somehow she found her voice and lied jerkily, 'I'd rather you didn't.'

'OK,' he said, and kissed her again. This time there was nothing light or fleeting about it.

When, without conscious volition, her lips parted beneath the light pressure of his, he deepened the kiss until her head was reeling and her very soul had lost its way.

He could feel her trembling and, sensing that she was his for the taking, he suggested softly, 'My apartment is quite close to here. Will you come up for a nightcap?'

Somehow she found her voice and objected huskily, 'It's late. I should get to bed.'

'Exactly what I had in mind…' he murmured.

She didn't dare look at him.

'With so much chemistry between us…' He let the sentence tail off.

But then he didn't need to say any more. Sex with him would be good, she knew that instinctively. Better than good. Mind-blowing.

Heat running through her, she said, 'I've never gone in for one-night stands,' and was uncomfortably aware that she sounded stuffy and old-fashioned.

Raising a dark brow, he asked, 'Who said anything about a one-night stand? I have the distinct feeling that having you in my arms for a million and one nights wouldn't be enough.'

Struggling to close her mind to the seduction in his voice and words, she looked down at her lap. For once in her life she was sorely tempted to do what Eve was always telling her to do, and live a little.

But the guilt that had been her albatross now became her saviour, reminding her that she couldn't afford—either financially or emotionally—to get involved with this man.

Taking a deep, steadying breath, she said, 'I don't want to go to bed with you. I'd like to go home, please.'

CHAPTER TWO

MADELINE braced herself, expecting him to be angry, to try and persuade her to change her mind, but, showing no signs of temper or disappointment, Rafe said evenly, 'Very well. If that's what you want.'

Relieved that he'd accepted her decision, that she'd won so easily, she made an effort to relax her taut muscles.

The relief turned out to be premature, as he returned to the attack.

'Have lunch with me tomorrow?' Before she could answer, he swept on, 'According to the forecast, it's going to be another lovely day. We could go for a drive, and picnic in an idyllic spot I know.'

'I'm afraid I can't.'

'You're not working tomorrow, are you?' he questioned.

'No. But I've a lot to do.' In a rush, she added, 'Saturday mornings I clean the flat, and then I do some shopping.'

She always bought a selection of small gifts for her mother, before catching the two-thirty bus to the nursing home.

He raised dark brows. 'Surely housework and shopping can wait? While this good weather holds, having a drive in the country and a picnic would be a lot more fun.'

Thinking of what had happened to her mother and Colin,

and feeling the black taste of guilt in her mouth, she said sharply, 'There's a lot more to life than just having fun.'

Then, seeing the shadow that had fallen across his face, and regretting lashing out, she touched his sleeve. 'I'm sorry. That wasn't very gracious of me.'

'No.' He covered her hand with his. 'But you don't have to be gracious with me. I'd much prefer honesty…'

She was surprised. None of the men she'd known had particularly valued honesty.

'Tell me why the idea of having a little fun upset you so much,' he pursued.

It wasn't something she could tell him.

It wasn't something she could bring herself to tell anyone. Not even Eve and Noel.

Pulling her hand free, she said jerkily, 'It isn't the idea of having fun… It's just that…' The words tailed off.

'You really can't stand the sight of me?'

She should have said yes, and be done with it. Instead, she said, 'No, it's nothing like that.'

'So what is it?'

'I—I don't have time for commitments…'

'I wasn't asking you to sign your life over to me,' he said mildly, 'merely to spend a few fleeting hours in my company. If you're busy Saturday morning, let's make it the afternoon.'

'I'm not free Saturday afternoon. I have to be out by two-thirty.'

'What time will you be home?'

Naturally truthful, she admitted, 'About six.'

'Then have dinner with me.'

Before she could think of an excuse, they were turning into Danetree Court, an old-fashioned block in a tree-lined square.

As they drew up outside her ground-floor flat, fumbling in her bag for her key, she said quickly, 'Don't bother to get out.'

Ignoring her injunction, Rafe asked the driver to wait and

accompanied her across the pavement. In the amber glow from the street lamp he unlocked the door and handed her back the key.

'Thank you.' Dropping it into her bag, she slipped inside and turned to face him.

He was standing so close that she could feel the warmth of his body and his breath stirring her hair.

She glanced up.

His mouth was only inches away. Just the thought of it touching hers again sent shivers down her spine and brought her out in goose-pimples.

She backed a step. 'And thank you for a very nice evening. I've had a lovely time.'

'I'm pleased you've enjoyed it.' Then, as though it was all settled, 'I thought we'd go to Annabel's tomorrow evening…'

She hesitated, knowing full well she should stop this thing in its tracks but wanting desperately to see him again.

Looking into her face, seeing her waver, he added firmly, 'I'll pick you up at seven-thirty.'

Though common sense told her she was being a fool, she agreed, 'All right.'

When he lifted a quizzical brow at her lack of enthusiasm, her voice unsteady, she added, 'I'll look forward to it… Well, goodnight.'

He tilted his head to one side, a gesture she was coming to know. 'Rafe?'

'Rafe,' she echoed obediently. It was the first time she had used his name.

'Goodnight, Madeleine. Sleep well.'

'Goodnight,' she said again.

He didn't turn away as she had expected. Instead he stood quite motionless, watching her.

She knew she should step back and close the door, but, fascinated by the unnerving stillness that generated so much sexual tension, she was still rooted to the spot when he bent and kissed her.

This time his mouth was not only sweet, but also *familiar*. His arms went around her, and he drew her close. His kiss was firm and masterful and when he sought to deepen it her lips parted as though there was no help for it.

The last obstacle removed, his mouth began to move against hers in a sizzling kiss that melted her last defences as easily as a blowtorch melted butter.

He tasted like ambrosia. Her stomach clenched and her heart began to race wildly, while desire dried her throat and ran like red-hot lava through her bloodstream.

She was no longer capable of thinking straight when, a few seconds later, he freed her mouth and, his voice husky, murmured, 'You're the most beautiful thing I've ever seen. I can't wait to feel your naked body against mine, to make love to you…'

Looking up into his shadowy face, she knew she ought to send him away. But she couldn't.

'Is that what you want?' he murmured.

She nodded silently and, her breathing shallow and ragged, waited impatiently while he went to pay off the taxi.

He came back and, taking her chin in his hand, lifted her face and began to kiss her again, kisses sweeter than wine, as he eased them inside and closed the door.

In the gloom, he continued to kiss her while he removed the clasp that held her hair. She heard his little murmur of satisfaction as the silky mass tumbled around her shoulders and he ran his fingers through it.

Then his hands slipped to the warmth of her nape and began to travel over her, tracing her shoulders, her ribcage, her slender waist, the flare of her hips and the curve of her firm buttocks.

'I've never met a women I wanted so much,' he murmured against her lips.

His touch was all she had ever hoped for or needed, and above his softly spoken words she could hear his heart beating. Or was it her own?

Caught up in a whirl of sensual delight, on a flight to the stars, she was hearing things, tasting things, feeling things that she had never heard or tasted or felt before.

While he continued to kiss her he unbuttoned her blouse and, unhooking the fastening of her bra, slipped one hand inside. Her breast fitted neatly into his palm. Enjoying the warm weight of it, he brushed his thumb over the velvety nipple and felt it firm beneath his touch. Shudders of pleasure running through her, she gasped deep in her throat. Hearing that muffled sound and interpreting it correctly, he bent his head to take the other nipple in his mouth and suckle until her whole body was on fire with longing.

When she could stand no more she pushed him away and, taking his hand, urged him towards the bedroom.

As the door closed behind them, the small voice of reason warned her that she was acting completely out of character. Acting like a fool.

But, having jumped into the deep end, she was in over her head and unwilling to be saved. Brushing reason aside, she moved to close the slatted window blind and shut out the night.

Turning to him, she saw the gleam of his eyes in the semi-darkness before he switched on the bedside lamp, flooding that part of the room in amber light.

On the dressing table close by was a framed snapshot of a smiling, fair-haired man.

Reaching out, Rafe picked it up and, his voice a little wary, asked, 'Is this your husband?'

She answered distractedly, 'Oh, no, that's Noel. He's out in the Middle East. In the oil fields.'

'An ex-lover?'

'A friend.'

Rafe replaced the photograph with care, and turned to gaze at her.

She had expected him to skip over the preliminaries and hurry her into bed, but with no suggestion of haste he said softly, 'I want to look at you. Take off your clothes for me.'

As though under a spell, she began to take off her suit and blouse. But modesty once ingrained was hard to dislodge, and, aware as she was of his appreciative gaze, the lick of flame in his eyes, her cheeks were hot as she stripped off her panties.

When she straightened and stood before him naked, he made a half-smothered sound deep in his throat, a very male sound, and without taking his eyes off her for an instant began to divest himself of his own shoes and clothing.

As she watched him discard his dark silk boxer shorts, it was her turn to smother the gasp that rose in her throat. Too turned on to move, she swallowed hard, her stomach tightening with anticipation.

'Come here,' he said.

When she obeyed, he lifted her onto the bed and stretched out beside her. Then, propping himself on one elbow, he leaned over her and, his hand fondling her breast, he said softly, 'You're exquisite. The loveliest thing I've ever seen.'

Colin had been an unexciting lover, with a low sex drive and little skill. Not only had he preferred to make love in the dark, but also he had never told her she was beautiful, nor had he caressed her in that way.

Rather, he had avoided touching her, as though he found the idea of enjoying sex something to be slightly ashamed of.

Rafe obviously had no such inhibitions.

Inhaling the fragrance of her skin, he murmured, 'You smell as fresh and delightful as apple blossom,' before his mouth began to roam over her.

She shivered deliciously as his unshaven jaw rasped against the smooth skin of her flat stomach.

When he had kissed and tasted every inch of her golden flesh, his mouth returned to pleasure her breasts while his fingers found the nest of pale, silky curls and began to explore further. Shivering, she gave herself up to the sensations those skilful fingers were engendering.

It wasn't long, however, before the exquisite torment grew too much to bear and she writhed under the lash of pleasure while desire rode her, digging in its spurs so that she began to make little whimpering sounds deep in her throat.

He paused, then, drawing her back against him, spoon-fashion, he eased her hips towards him before returning his hands to her breasts.

Just at first he was careful, as though gauging her reaction. Then he began to thrust more strongly, building a tension that spiralled and grew until the sensations, almost too great to be borne, peaked, and stars exploded inside her head.

Hearing her little gasping cries with pleasure, he held her there, drawing out the moment, until he too was caught up in the surging excitement.

For a while they lay together quietly while their heart rates and breathing returned to normal. Then he drew away, and, turning her to face him, gathered her close and kissed her tenderly.

Knowing she'd been married, he had been somewhat thrown, partly by her obvious shyness, and partly by her instinctive reaction to their lovemaking. Her obvious pleasure had been followed by what he could have sworn was *gratitude*. Frowning, he wondered if her husband had been clumsy and lacking skill, or simply uncaring.

Seeing that frown, she asked a shade anxiously, 'I hope you weren't disappointed?'

'Anything but,' he assured her.

Then, picking up her very real concern, he kissed her and, leaning his forehead against hers, told her with soft emphasis, 'You're very special, and I'm immensely flattered that you let me into your bed.'

Feeling her relax, with a little sigh of relief he settled her head on his shoulder. She felt limp as a rag doll. The power and intensity of his lovemaking had left her exhausted, totally drained, yet at the same time full of bliss, brimming with rapture.

Never for a moment had she imagined love could be like this—and yes, it *was* love—never imagined that this strength of feeling could take root and blossom so quickly. It wasn't just the result of sexual deprivation, nor was it simply the chemistry between them. This was different. This was more. Much more.

They seemed to meet on every level, physical, mental and emotional. And as she slid into sleep she found herself thinking that if she searched the world over she would never find a man who was more right for her.

The same thought was in her mind when she stirred and surfaced slowly, her body relaxed and satisfied, a quiet happiness singing through her.

She was in love, truly in love, for the very first time. It was a big risk, letting herself fall so hard and so fast for a man she had only just met.

But she couldn't say she hadn't known what she was doing. Well aware that she was vulnerable, well aware that she was teetering on the brink of falling for him, well aware that making love with him could easily push her over, she had walked into it with her eyes wide open.

And it had been wonderful beyond words. She had never felt so utterly content. Not even her guilt over Colin could spoil things, or alter the way she felt about Rafe.

Sighing, she stretched out a hand to touch him, but she was alone. Jolted wide awake, she opened her eyes to find he was standing by the bed fully dressed, a cup of tea in his hand.

'I'm sorry to wake you, but I thought it best if I left early.'

He set the cup on the bedside cabinet and smiled down at her. The blind was still closed, but even in the half-light his thickly lashed green eyes were brilliant, and with his hair a little rumpled, a dark stubble adorning his jaw, he looked irresistibly virile and attractive.

Her heart doing strange things, she pushed herself into a sitting position.

'What I'd really like to do,' he went on, 'is stay and make love to you until such a time as the sight of a strange man leaving your flat wouldn't raise a single eyebrow...'

Just his words made her go hot all over and sent a surge of desire running through her.

'But bearing in mind what you said about having a lot to do, I'm restraining the urge...'

Disappointment pricked sharp as a thorn.

'I'll pick you up at seven-thirty.'

He stooped and kissed her, a lingering kiss, as if he couldn't bear to leave her. She was on the verge of begging him to stay when he straightened and strode to the door.

An instant later he was gone.

For a moment or two she felt empty and lost—*bereft*—as if the whole thing had been nothing but a wonderful dream. But the cup of tea sitting by her elbow was tangible proof, not only that he was no dream, but also that he'd cared enough to think about her. Gladness returning, she reached for the cup and took a sip. Only the day to get through and she would be seeing him again.

Excitement and anticipation buoying her up, the morning passed quite quickly, and even her afternoon visit to the nursing home didn't seem quite so fraught as usual. For the first time in what seemed an age, happiness was crowding out guilt. Or at least masking it.

By a quarter past seven that evening, showered, dressed and lightly made-up, Madeleine was ready and waiting. Standing by the window, she watched as a silver Porsche drew up by the kerb promptly at seven-thirty, and Rafe jumped out. He looked breathtakingly handsome in well-cut evening clothes, and she wondered if she was underdressed for Annabel's.

Taking deep breaths to calm herself, she let him ring the bell before picking up her evening purse and going to open the door.

He smiled at her. 'Ready?'

Madeleine nodded. 'Will I do?' she asked a shade anxiously.

His glance swept over her from head to toe.

She was wearing a simple black dress that clung lovingly to her slender curves and set off her flawless, pale gold skin. Her blonde hair was taken up in a gleaming coil that served to emphasise her pure bone structure, and in her neat lobes were small gold hoops.

A light in his eyes, he said, 'You look stunning,' and bent his dark head to kiss her.

Her heart leapt in her breast, and she knew he held everything she was, everything she hoped for, in the palm of his hand.

It was a beautiful evening, warm and still, and she could smell roses in the heart of town as she was escorted to the car.

When she was settled, he slid in beside her and started the engine. As they left the square behind them and joined the evening queue of traffic, he queried lightly, 'Missed me?'

The true answer was yes, but she said primly, 'I haven't had time.'

'So what have you been doing all day?'

'Nothing very exciting. I spent most of the morning cleaning and shopping.'

'But you went out in the afternoon? Anywhere nice?'

Flustered by the question, she said, 'No, not particularly.' She had meant to sound casual, but it came out as defensive, and she bit her lip.

Intrigued by her tone, he wondered what she was hiding. Deciding not to push it—he'd find out when he knew her better—he changed tack.

'What made you decide to become a physiotherapist?'

She relaxed, glad to chat about her work. 'You might call it following in my father's footsteps. Physiotherapy was his chosen profession, and it was widely acknowledged that he had healing hands. When I was a child he became prominent in his field, and so much in demand that he turned into a workaholic.'

'So you didn't see much of him?' Rafe questioned.

'No.' There was a remembered hint of sadness. 'When he wasn't at his consulting rooms in Baker Street, he was often in the States giving lecture tours.'

'Why the States? Any particular reason?'

'My father's American by birth. He was brought up and had done his early training in Boston.'

'So you're half American? Any relatives over there?' he asked.

'Just an aunt and uncle we used to visit. They were always delighted to see us.' Madeleine smiled as she reminisced.

Rafe asked no further questions, and they lapsed into silence until the Porsche drew up outside the famous basement entrance in Berkeley Square.

When he had helped her out, he handed the keys to the doorman and they made their way down the steps and in through a door at the bottom.

'Good evening, Mr Lombard. Nice to see you.' Clearly well-known, Rafe was welcomed inside.

As he signed in he was greeted by a couple who looked

inclined to attach themselves, until he said with smooth politeness, 'Well, if you'll excuse us?' and led Madeleine away.

When they were out of earshot, he added, 'Jo and Tom are very nice, but I wanted you all to myself tonight.'

She flushed with pleasure.

There was a mere handful of people in the bar, even fewer in the restaurant, and the dance floor was empty, its dark mirrors reflecting nothing.

'It doesn't get busy until later, so we'll have plenty of time to dine in comfort and then we can dance later.'

Just the thought of being held in his arms made her temperature rise even more.

When they were settled at a table and had been given menus, he asked, 'Is there anything in particular you fancy?'

Wanting only to watch his face in the candlelight, she shook her head. 'You order for me.'

The order given, they were sipping an aperitif when he reached across the table and, taking her slim but strong hand, examined it.

'You said your father had healing hands. Have you?'

'I'm afraid not,' she said honestly. 'Nor have I my father's sheer dedication.'

'So you're not a committed career woman?' He glanced up and met her gaze.

'Not really. I could be just as happy being a wife and mother.'

'At the risk of sounding chauvinistic, I find that highly commendable in this materialistic age. Most of the women I've met have been career-orientated. Being 'just' a wife and mother comes a very poor second to their independence. No wonder so many men feel threatened…'

His white smile flashed suddenly. 'Don't get me wrong, I wouldn't want a brainless, compliant woman, no matter how beautiful she was, nor would I want a clinging vine…'

'What *would* you want?' She laughed.

'An intelligent, independently minded woman who was capable of standing beside me as my equal. Yet a woman who would be willing to put her home and family before her career.'

Had he stayed single because he couldn't find the right kind of woman? she wondered. Or was that just an excuse so he could go on playing the field?

As though he knew exactly what she was thinking, he added, 'Someone with all those qualities isn't easy to find. That's one of the reasons I haven't been in a hurry to marry.'

'Then you intend to?' The instant the words were out she wished them unsaid, and the warm colour rose in her cheeks.

A hint of amusement in his voice, he said, 'Oh yes, I fully intend to…'

To Madeleine's relief the arrival of the first course provided a welcome diversion, and during the rest of what proved to be a very enjoyable meal Rafe kept the conversation light and general.

They had reached the coffee stage before he returned to more personal matters, by asking, 'Do you enjoy your work at the clinic?'

'Yes. Though of course it's just a temporary post, and part-time.'

'You have private patients as well?'

'Some. But by the time this job ends I'm hoping to have more,' Madeleine said, taking a sip of her coffee.

'Do you treat children?' Rafe asked.

'Oh, yes. At the moment I'm visiting a young boy who injured his knee playing football. Why do you ask?'

'My sister, Diane, and her husband, Stuart, have a problem. A couple of months ago their ten-year-old daughter, Katie, was quite badly injured when she fell from her horse. Since leaving hospital Katie has been treated at home, but it seems she's grown to dislike her present physiotherapist and has refused to have any further treatment. Would you be willing to take a look at her?'

A little flustered, Madeleine agreed, 'Of course. If you think I'll be able to help.'

'If Katie takes to you, and I can't imagine she won't, you could be the answer to all our prayers… More coffee?'

'I don't think so, thank you.'

Rafe smiled a dazzling smile and asked. 'Then would you like to dance?'

The club had started to fill up, and there were several couples already on the floor.

Madeleine's eyes lit up. 'Yes, I'd love to.'

Even in her own ears her words sounded eager and breathless, and as he took her hand and led her onto the floor she wondered where the old cool and composed Madeleine had gone.

Though it was a long time since she had been on a dance floor, she had always enjoyed dancing. But this was something special.

He was a good dancer, light on his feet and with a purely masculine grace. As he held her to his heart, his cheek against her hair, they moved round the floor as though made for each other.

For Madeleine the rest of the evening passed in a kind of dream as, without speaking, just enjoying the music and the closeness, they danced every dance.

When the floor started to get crowded, Rafe murmured in her ear, 'About ready to go?'

She nodded, a little shiver of excitement running down her spine. She hadn't allowed herself to think any further than dining and dancing at Annabel's, but now the evening was over and the night lay ahead.

When she was settled in the Porsche, he turned to look directly into her eyes. 'I shared your bed last night. Will you come to Denver Court tonight and share mine?'

A betraying catch in her voice, she agreed lightly, 'That seems only fair.'

As they drew up outside the imposing tower-block complex and he helped her out, one of the night security staff came hurrying over.

'Evening, Mr Lombard... Anything I can do for you?'

'Could you put the car away, please, Jim?' A folded note changed hands.

His arm around her waist, Rafe escorted Madeleine into the building and across the pale marble-floored foyer to the lift.

On the top floor they stepped out into a wide, luxuriously carpeted area with a white and gold decor and extravagant arrangements of fresh flowers.

When he let them into his apartment and flicked on the lights, she saw that he occupied one of the corner penthouse suites. From the spacious and attractive L-shaped living room, French windows led onto a walled patio and garden.

She gasped as she looked around her, taking in the luxurious surroundings. Rafe smiled and bent to touch his lips to the warmth of her nape, before asking, 'Would you like a nightcap?'

Shivering a little at the caress, and impatient for the pleasures to come, she shook her head.

Taking her hand in his, he led her through to a large *en suite* bedroom with pale walls and a thundercloud-blue carpet and curtains.

Opening a connecting door into a similar room decorated in ivory tones, he suggested, 'If you'd like to use the guest-room facilities you'll find everything there you need.'

In the well-appointed bathroom there was indeed everything a guest could want, including slippers and a white towelling robe.

She found herself wondering how often he brought his women back here.

It was an uncomfortable thought, and she pushed it hastily

away. This might only be another brief and casual affair as far as *he* was concerned, but for her it was special, a once-in-a-lifetime love affair, no matter how short a time it lasted.

When she had cleaned her teeth and showered, she brushed out her long, silky hair and, a little shy, put on the towelling robe before making her way back to Rafe's room.

He was just emerging from his bathroom, stark naked apart from a towel slung round his neck that he was using one-handed to rub his dark hair.

As she hesitated in the doorway, tossing aside the towel, he held out both hands. 'Come here.'

Loving that touch of arrogance, she went to him, and was rewarded with a lingering kiss.

He had shaved, and she could smell the fresh, spicy scent of his cologne. Eyes still closed, she put up a hand and stroked his smooth cheek.

'Mmm…' she murmured.

Nuzzling his face against her throat, he said, 'I intend to kiss every inch of you, and bristles can play havoc with delicate skin.'

Untying the belt of her robe, he slid his hands inside and, like a blind man reading Braille, ran his fingers over her slender body, savouring the purely tactile pleasure.

It was strangely erotic, and by the time his hands returned to her breasts she was quivering all over. When his thumbs brushed lightly across the sensitive nipples, she gasped.

As he continued to tease, soon aroused to fever-pitch, she pressed her hips against his.

But, refusing to be hurried, he said, 'We've got all night. Plenty of time to take things slow and easy, to ravish you, in the best sense of the word.'

She wondered how he could be so patient, so willing to wait for his own pleasure.

As though reading her mind, he said softly, 'Your body

responds so delightfully to my every touch, it makes the pleasure mutual.'

He put his mouth to her breast and laved the nipple with his tongue. 'You like that, don't you?'

She shuddered, and, holding his dark head between her hands, breathed, 'Yes, but I don't think I can stand much more…'

'Oh, I think you can.'

When he finally lifted her onto the bed and stretched out beside her, she was almost mindless, poised on the brink.

He stoked a caressing hand down her slender figure and, finding the warm, silky skin of her inner thighs, used a single long finger to tip her over. Her whole body bucked convulsively, and she lay quivering and helpless until the exquisite sensations began to die away.

She felt a little *triste*. She had wanted to make love *with* him, to share the experience, to know he was feeling the same delight and joy she was feeling.

When she opened dazed eyes, he was watching her.

Smiling at her, as though he understood perfectly, he said, 'It's all right,' and with those skilful hands he proceeded to reawaken the desire she had thought sated.

Then slowly, very slowly, as though to draw every last ounce of pleasure out of it, he made love to her, building up a molten core of heat, a spiralling tension, until the tension snapped and sent them both rocketing into space.

She drifted back to earth to find his dark head was lying on her breast and his hand holding hers. It was one of the sweetest sensations she had ever felt.

Her heart overflowing with love and gratitude she lay quietly enjoying their closeness until he moved away and, turning onto his back, gathered her against him and settled her head on his shoulder.

CHAPTER THREE

AFTER a night OF love-making, it was almost ten o'clock when Madeleine woke. She was alone in the big bed, but just as that fact registered the door opened and Rafe came in carrying a tray.

His dark hair was still damp from the shower, and he was wearing a short, navy-blue silk robe. 'Good morning.' He smiled lazily as she pushed herself upright. 'I thought we'd be decadent and have breakfast in bed.'

He put the tray on the bedside table and, leaning over to kiss her, remarked wickedly, 'After the night we've just spent, I don't know how you can look so beautiful and fresh.'

'I'm happy,' she said simply. She had never thought she would say those words again.

He smiled at her. 'Happiness suits you.'

As he sat on the bed and fed her toast and scrambled eggs and coffee, his voice casual, Rafe suggested, 'Tell me some more about yourself.'

Instantly uneasy, she said, 'There's not a great deal to tell.'

Sensing that unease, and wondering what was causing it, he decided to go slowly. 'Do your parents still live in London?'

'They got divorced when I was twelve.'

'Presumably it was your father's dedication to work that caused the break-up.'

'Yes. Though my mother loved him passionately, eventually she got fed up with him never being there for us.' Madeleine turned her head away from him.

'Was it an amicable parting?'

'As amicable as these things ever can be.'

Rafe probed further, 'But you must have missed him?'

'Yes, I did, and I don't think my mother ever really got over it.' She felt her eyes begin to water, but she smiled as she looked up at Rafe.

'She didn't marry again?'

'No. I believe she still loves him. Certainly there was never anyone else.'

'Do you still see him?'

Madeleine shook her head. 'Some time after the divorce he remarried and went to live in Los Angeles. We haven't had any contact for years.'

Then, wanting to escape from the spotlight, she said quickly, 'Now it's your turn to tell me something about yourself.'

His face straight, he replied, 'There's not a great deal to tell.' He laughed and kissed her, before beginning, 'I lost my father when I was twelve. A year after he died, my mother married again. Her new husband was an ex-army officer.'

'Did you all get on as a family?'

'Diane, who's seven years older than me, was away at university, so that left just the three of us, and unfortunately my stepfather and I *didn't* get along. I resented him taking my father's place and showed it, which, with hindsight, must have made life extremely difficult for my mother. My stepfather was a strict disciplinarian and after he'd whacked me a couple of times for what he termed insolence, I began to seriously hate his guts.' Rafe paused for a moment before continuing.

'Things went from bad to worse, and the whacks changed to beatings. On the final occasion, when he began to lay into me with his belt, my mother tried to intervene. He pushed her out of the way so roughly that she stumbled and fell. I saw red and went for him. I wasn't quite fourteen at the time.'

Her aquamarine eyes full of concern, Madeleine asked, 'What happened?'

Matter-of-factly, he said, 'I managed to split his lip before ending up in Casualty.'

As she winced he added, 'I think he may have been genuinely sorry afterwards. But it was patently obvious that things couldn't go on like that, so I was hastily packed off to live with my godparents.'

Madeleine reached out to touch his arm. 'Were you very upset?'

'For a time I was very bitter,' he admitted. 'Though my godparents were amazing.'

'Had they any children of their own?'

'One daughter, Fiona. But they had always hoped for a son, and were only too delighted to have me.'

'Fiona wasn't jealous at all?'

His face softened. 'Oh, no. We got to be very close. In fact for a while she hero-worshipped me. She was nearly three years younger than me, and I always called her my kid sister.'

'So it was a good move?'

'Oh, yes. The whole family treated me exactly like their own, and I was very happy with them until I went up to Oxford. My godfather died eighteen months ago and it was like losing a father...

'But that's enough doom and gloom—let's talk about something else. What shall we do for the rest of the day? Would you like to—'

'I can't,' she broke in desperately. On Sundays she always had lunch at the nursing home, and spent the rest of the afternoon and evening there. 'I mean, I'm already going out.'

When she made no effort to elaborate, he asked, 'What time do you need to start?'

'In about an hour.'

'Then as soon as you've showered and dressed, I'll take you home.' Though his voice was even, she knew he was vexed by her reticence, but she couldn't bring herself to tell him about her mother. He was sure to ask questions that, burdened with guilt, she didn't want to answer.

His profile cool and aloof, he drove through the Sunday streets in silence. She longed to break that silence, but could think of nothing to say.

When he drew up outside her flat and, still without speaking, helped her out, she felt a sudden panic in case this was the end.

What would she do if he simply drove away?

As though to keep her guessing, he unlocked her door and handed her back the key, before asking, 'Are you free tomorrow evening?'

'Yes,' she said eagerly.

'Then if you like, I'll take you to see Katie and her parents. I've already mentioned your name to them.'

'There's just one thing...' Madeleine began a shade awkwardly.

Reading her hesitation, he said, 'You prefer to keep your private and professional lives separate?'

'Yes, I do.'

'That's fine by me. All they know up to now is that you're the physiotherapist who checked me out, and we can keep it that way. I'll pick you up at six-thirty, and afterwards we can have dinner.'

Madeleine liked Rafe's sister and brother-in-law on sight. Over drinks on the sunny terrace of their Surrey home she learnt that Diane, with her brother's seal-dark hair and green eyes, was a lawyer, and Stuart, a pleasant, easy-going man, worked as an architect.

They both doted on their only daughter and were over the moon when Katie took an immediate liking to Madeleine, and agreed to have further treatment.

The liking was mutual. Madeleine instantly lost her heart to the quiet, sensitive child, with her long dark hair, her big brown eyes and shy smile.

Over the next few weeks, with regular treatments, Katie's condition improved enormously, and a strong bond developed between her and Madeleine.

Rafe was delighted for everyone's sake, but he stayed well out of things and, though his and Madeleine's relationship grew and blossomed, it was never mentioned.

They spent as much time with one another as possible, dancing, dining, talking, simply being together.

Several times, while the good weather held, he barbecued for them on his patio. Afterwards, safe from prying eyes, they made sweet, delectable love in the sun.

As the days and weeks passed and Madeleine got to know him better, her happiness increased. Apart from his physical attributes and his prowess as a lover, he proved to be even-tempered and generous, an intelligent, stimulating companion, always sensitive to her needs.

She knew that never in her lifetime would she find another man who suited her so well, and, eternally grateful, she said many a prayer of thanks to the goddess of destiny for the miracle that had brought him into her life.

Only her visits to the nursing home cast a shadow. Rafe said nothing openly, but she knew he was ruffled by her un-explained absences. Even a little jealous of whom she might be meeting.

Each time she tried to tell him the truth guilt made the

words stick in her throat, and she chickened out. But one of these days, she promised herself, she *would* find the courage to tell him everything.

In the meantime, though she still spent most of Sunday at the nursing home, she had changed her Saturday visit to the morning—struggling with the shopping and housework when she could—to leave the afternoon free.

That Saturday afternoon they had something very special planned. Jonathan Cass was one of her favourite artists, and Rafe had accepted an invitation to a one-day private showing of Cass's new, and so far unseen, works.

He had arranged to pick her up at twelve-thirty so they could have lunch together before going on to the Piccadilly gallery, and she left the nursing home earlier than usual to make certain she was home in good time.

She was only just back when the phone rang.

Sounding tense, unlike himself, Rafe said, 'Some urgent business has cropped up. Would you mind very much if I picked you up after lunch?'

'Of course not.'

Sounding relieved, he said, 'Then I'll see you about two.'

It had been a damp, grey morning, and by two o'clock it was pelting down with rain.

Rafe was always on time—she had never known him to be late—and as the hands of the clock moved with maddening slowness—two-fifteen, two-thirty, a quarter to three—and he failed to arrive, she began to get anxious and jumpy.

As she stood staring blindly out into the wet, windswept square, watching the raindrops run down the windowpane like tears, she saw the ghost of his face blurry in the glass and felt a queer foreboding.

Oh, dear God, suppose something had happened to him? The panicky thought made her heart begin to race uncomfortably fast.

Don't be a fool, she chided herself. Of course nothing had happened to him. No doubt he'd just been held up. But if that was the case, why hadn't he phoned? It would have only taken a moment to reassure her.

After waiting until three-thirty without hearing from him she called his mobile, only to find it was switched off. In desperation she tried his flat at Denver Court, but it rang hollow and empty, until the answering machine picked up her call.

By the time five o'clock arrived, convinced that her worst fears had been realised, she was a mass of jangling nerves. She was wondering agitatedly whom she could contact, when she saw his car pull up outside. The rush of relief was so great that it made her feel giddy and light-headed.

He had his own key by now, and she stood, her knees trembling so much they would hardly support her, while he crossed the streaming pavement and let himself in. She wanted to run to him, but she could neither move nor speak.

'I'm sorry I couldn't get here any sooner.' As he spoke he took off his coat and hung it up.

When he turned she noticed some angry-looking marks on his face, as though a cat had raked its claws down his cheek.

'What have you done to your face?'

'It's just a scratch,' he said dismissively.

Taking a deep, steadying breath, she remarked, 'I wondered what had happened to you.'

'I was unavoidably detained.'

She waited for some kind of explanation, but he said nothing further.

After so much anxiety, his casual dismissal of the subject caught her on the raw.

Seeing her mouth tighten, he said, 'We can still go to the gallery this evening.'

'It's not that,' she assured him stiffly. 'I was worried to death about you. I just wish you'd given me a ring.'

'I'm afraid my mobile went on the blink.'

The obvious excuse did nothing to help matters.

'Forgive me?' Seeing her set face, he smiled. 'Oh, dear, obviously not.'

His eyes fixed on her mouth, he bent his head to kiss her. She moved back a step.

He sighed. 'And here I've been, waiting all day to kiss you. Waiting all day just to touch you, to take you to bed and make love to you.'

Angry with him for his cavalier attitude, she looked at him stonily.

'In that case, I'll have to resort to a spot of friendly persuasion.'

Catching the lapels of her jacket, he pulled her towards him. Then, one hand beneath her chin, he lifted her face to meet his kiss.

It wasn't until his lips touched hers that she realised just how urgent was her need to have him kiss her. Just how much she needed to be reassured that he was really here, to be with her.

But, unwilling to let him know it, she tried her utmost to hide how she felt. Though she badly wanted to, she refused to put her arms round his neck, refused to melt against him as she normally did.

Even so, they were standing so close she could feel the warmth of his body, the ripple of his muscles, the firmness of his flesh.

His hand slid up and down her spine in a restless movement that told her he didn't like restraining himself, but was doing it anyway while he waited for some sign that he was forgiven.

After a time, when none was forthcoming, he lifted his mouth enough to murmur huskily, 'Are you persuaded yet?'

Her anger having drained away, she answered, 'Not yet; keep trying.'

His lips curved into a smile before his arms closed around her and he kissed her again.

Unable to resist him any longer, she reached up slowly, her fingertips tenderly tracing the scratches, before her palm cupped the hard planes of his cheek.

She heard his indrawn breath before he covered her hand with his own and, carrying it to his lips, kissed the palm.

Her whole being melted with love for him, and she wondered, how on earth had she managed to live before she met him?

When she tugged her hand free he frowned, a frown that changed to a glint of satisfaction as her fingers began to undo his shirt buttons.

It was only later that she realised she ought to have pressed him for an explanation first, but how could she, when so many times she had failed to give *him* one?

His need urgent, he swept her up in his arms and carried her through to the bedroom. When he had swiftly undressed her and lifted her onto the bed, he stripped off his own clothes.

Though she had seen him naked many times, she caught her breath yet again. He was a magnificent male animal, and she was his chosen mate. It was as wonderfully simple, as down to earth, as that.

Mostly he was a slow, skilful lover who took his time and enjoyed pleasuring her, building up the intensity until often she was gasping and writhing, hardly able to bear all the exquisite sensations he was engendering.

But now he wasted no time on foreplay, and trembling enough to rouse him even more, she accepted his weight eagerly.

She could hear his quickened breathing, feel the thump of his heart, and knowing she had caused it gave her pleasure.

Briefly she was pliant beneath him, waiting. Then she was taut as a drawn bow string as he drove hard and fast, carrying them both to a shattering climax.

She experienced a complete losing of self, then a gradual

gathering back as they lay in an erotic tangle of limbs, both breathing as if they'd just run a race.

After a while he lifted himself away and, leaning over her, brushed a loose tendril of silky blonde hair away from her flushed cheek.

'All right?' His expression held a mixture of concern and tenderness.

'Of course,' she assured him. 'Why shouldn't I be?'

'Well, I wasn't very gentle.'

His words made her think, made her suddenly appreciate that normally he was *careful* with her. But something—that brief touch of discord perhaps?—had thrown him off balance.

'You don't have to treat me like porcelain,' she told him a shade tartly. 'I won't break.'

Suddenly he was laughing. 'Are you trying to tell me you prefer it hard and fast to slow and easy? Well, well, well…'

'I'm not trying to tell you anything of the kind. I like…' She broke off and, feeling her colour rise, tried to wriggle free.

Putting an arm either side of her, he said silkily, 'Do go on. It's about time you opened up and told me. What *do* you like? I'm always willing to oblige.'

He was in a strange mood, she thought, and accused, 'You're trying to embarrass me.'

'Succeeding too, if the way you're blushing is anything to go by,' he said arrogantly.

Pushing herself up, she made another, more determined, attempt to escape.

He foiled her by the simple expedient of pulling her elbows from beneath her.

'Don't be shy. Tell me.'

'Rafe, *please*…'

'That's my intention as soon as I know what pleases you the most…'

When she remained silent, he sighed. 'Oh, well, if you're

determined not to tell me, I'll just have to experiment and make my own judgement…'

'Not now.' She tried once more to sit up.

Pushing her gently back, he said, 'Now.'

Secure in the knowledge that all hunger was sated, she said, 'You'll be wasting your time.'

'I don't think so.'

She quivered like a plucked string under his hands as he effortlessly re-aroused her desire. Soon she was spinning in some crazy world of sublime sensations while his every touch, his seeking mouth and tongue added more…

When finally she lay limp and emotionally drained, he gathered her close and kissed her. 'Sleep now.'

After a short time she awoke refreshed to find he was up and dressed.

'If we have a quick meal at the Xanadu we've still got time to go to the gallery.'

'We don't *have* to go.'

'I know you want to.' Bending down to kiss her, he added, 'And I don't want you to miss out on anything that gives you pleasure.'

As she showered and dressed, she thought—as she'd thought before and was to think many times in the coming weeks—how lucky she was to have Rafe. With a quiet but radiant happiness, she found herself daring to anticipate the day when he would tell her he loved her and ask her to be his wife.

Then, one golden evening in late September, a woman arrived at the clinic asking to speak to Madeleine on a matter of some urgency.

Presuming it was business, she agreed, and when a tall, good-looking brunette was shown in, she held out her hand with a friendly smile. 'Hello… I'm Madeleine Knight.'

The expression in her dark eyes unmistakably hostile, the newcomer, beautifully dressed and thin to the point of gauntness, ignored the proffered hand. 'And I'm Fiona Charn, Rafe's fiancée…'

Sitting down in the visitor's chair, she crossed slim, silk-clad legs. 'To put it bluntly, I gather that while I've been away this last time, he's been bedding you…'

Watching the hot colour pour into Madeleine's cheeks, Fiona added, 'But I'm wearing his ring.' She flashed a large, square-cut emerald.

Somehow Madeleine gathered herself enough to say jerkily, 'I had no idea he had a fiancée.'

'Oh, I don't blame *you* in particular. Rafe's always been a red-blooded man, and if it hadn't been you it would have been some other woman. He's extremely attractive to the opposite sex. Women throw themselves at him, so in a way one can't wonder that he takes advantage…

'But now I'm home it has to stop. Rafe's mine.'

Her voice sounding thin and tight, Madeleine said, 'If he's that kind of man I'm surprised you still want him.'

'Oh, I want him all right, so if you were thinking of suggesting that I set him free, forget it… For one thing he doesn't want out, and for another, we have a bargain…'

'A bargain?' Madeleine echoed.

'When it became clear that I was to be an only child, Daddy was bitterly disappointed. He held the old-fashioned belief that no mere woman could be expected to run a business empire successfully. Then Rafe came to live with us, and it was like a dream come true. The son he'd always wanted.

'Daddy was a wealthy man, but most of his money was tied up in the business and, to give him his due, he was concerned about my future.' Fiona paused, tossing her silken hair over her shoulder.

'After his first heart attack, he talked things over with Rafe and agreed to leave Charn Industries to him lock, stock and barrel if he would marry me and take care of me…'

Yes, Madeleine remembered being told that Rafe had inherited the Charn empire from his godfather.

'Rafe and I had been lovers for some time, so he was quite happy to make it legal. We'd have been married by now and there wouldn't have been a problem if I hadn't been diagnosed with a rare blood disorder. I've had to spend long periods in a private clinic undergoing treatment, which meant Rafe was left alone, and, as I say, he's a red-blooded man who needs a woman. Any woman.'

Her voice brittle, Fiona went on, 'Then I discovered I was pregnant, which made this last treatment more prolonged and complicated, and in the end I lost the baby…'

Shocked and horrified to think that she and Rafe had been lovers while his fiancée went through such an ordeal, Madeleine stood rooted to the spot, staring at her.

'But now I'm back home for good, and we'll be getting married fairly soon. I don't intend to let him stray, so I suggest you find yourself another man, preferably one that doesn't belong to some other woman.'

Getting to her feet, Fiona stalked out without a backward glance, leaving Madeleine devastated, shattered, her insides fractured into tiny pieces like a car's windscreen smashed with a hammer.

She was still standing staring blindly into space when Eve came in carrying the next patient's notes. 'Dear God!' she exclaimed, after a glance at her friend's face. 'You're as white as a sheet. What on earth's wrong?'

Madeleine focused with difficulty, and her voice impeded, said, 'Fiona Charn, the woman who just went out, is Rafe's fiancée.'

'What?'

'She's Rafe's fiancée,' Madeleine repeated.

Seeing her sway, and afraid she was going to faint, Eve pushed her into a chair.

'You're sure? You haven't got the wrong end of the stick or anything?'

'She was wearing his ring.'

'No! It can't be right; he loves you... I felt sure he did.' Eve was angry and indignant on her behalf. 'But if he's that kind of man, perhaps you're better off without him...'

She gave her friend a quick hug and, seeing the blankness of shock still on Madeleine's face, said, 'Look, why don't you go home? I'll tell Mrs Bond you're ill and get someone to fill in for you.'

'No... I'll be all right. I'd rather keep working. Just give me a few minutes.'

When Madeleine went home that evening, Eve insisted on going with her. 'Noel might well be out, and I don't think you should be alone,' she said soberly.

But Noel, who was just back from the Middle East and currently sleeping on Madeleine's bed-settee, *was* at home.

When he heard the news he was sympathetic, even angrier than his sister, and a great deal more vocal. 'I'd like to break the bastard's neck,' was one of his more restrained comments.

But as Madeleine pointed out bleakly, though Rafe had treated the woman who was to be his future wife with a callous disregard that was unforgivable, he had told *her* no lies. Promised *her* nothing.

He had never said he was free, never said he loved her or asked for her love. She had given it freely, and foolishly perhaps, *presumed* he was free, *presumed* he cared about her.

She couldn't have been more wrong. But perhaps, after what had happened to Colin and her mother, she didn't deserve to be happy. Perhaps it was poetic justice that Rafe hadn't loved her, any more than she had loved Colin... Perhaps this was what she deserved...

'Don't make excuses for him,' Noel broke into her thoughts. 'He's just been using you... I take it you won't be joining him in Paris?'

'No!' she said determinedly.

Rafe was in the French capital on business, and he had made all the arrangements for Madeleine to join him for a long weekend. It was a romantic trip she had been greatly looking forward to—staying on the Champs-Elysées, dining on the Bateaux Mouches, walking hand in hand down the Rue de Rivoli...

But now everything had changed.

'When he gets back,' Noel went on, 'face up to the swine and tell him what you think of him.'

'I can't,' she whispered.

How could she let Rafe see how heartbroken she was, how utterly devastated? It would be humiliating, mortifying. Somehow she had to walk away with at least her self-respect intact.

Guessing what was in her mind, Eve approved her decision. 'It might be best to let him think you don't care, that it doesn't mean a thing to you. At least that way you won't be just another scalp dangling from his belt...'

'So how are you going to get out of this Paris trip without letting him suspect the truth?' Noel asked.

'I don't know,' Madeleine said helplessly.

After the three of them had talked it over for a while, Eve exclaimed, 'I've got it! Send the brute a 'Dear John' email. Tell him you've met someone new and you're finishing with him.'

'I don't think that would work,' Madeleine demurred. 'He's only been in Paris two days—there hasn't been time for me to have met anyone else.'

'In that case make it someone you already know,' Eve said thoughtfully.

Madeleine shrugged. 'But I don't know anyone I could begin to pretend was a new lover…'

'What about me?' Noel asked. When Madeleine stared at him blankly, he said, 'Don't look at me like that, or you'll seriously damage my ego. Aren't I tanned and handsome, personable enough to play the part of your lover?'

'Of course, but—'

'Then all you have to do is tell the lowdown skunk that I'm the man you really care about. Go on to say that I've been away working, and now I'm back he's redundant, so to speak. That would do the trick, don't you think?'

'It might,' Madeleine admitted. 'He once saw a snapshot of you and wanted to know who it was. When I told him, he asked if you were an ex-lover. I said no, a friend.'

'That's fine, then. You wouldn't have been likely to admit to your current lover that I was more than just a friend, would you?

'Right…' He produced his laptop. 'Get cracking, and make it offhand enough to trample his masculine pride in the dust. That way you'll never have to set eyes on him again.'

After some input from both Eve and Noel, the short email read:

Noel has returned from the Middle East sooner than
I'd expected, so I'm afraid I won't be able to join you
in Paris after all.
Sorry it's a bit last-minute, but I'm sure you'll
be able to find someone else to take my place.
Thanks for all the good times.
Madeleine.

'That should do the trick,' Noel approved.

Eve agreed, and the email was duly sent.

It wasn't until after supper, when Eve had gone home and

Noel was settled on the bed-settee, that the full realisation of what she'd done struck her, and she gave way to the bitter unhappiness that crowded in.

Climbing into bed, she buried her face in the pillow and cried until she had no more tears left, before falling into an exhausted sleep.

Next morning when she awoke, Noel was already up, and as she tidied the bedding away and folded the settee she could hear the shower running.

Still in her night things, she was making coffee when he strolled into the kitchen with a towel knotted around his lean hips.

'Mmm...smells good.'

Madeleine had just turned to hand him a mug when she saw a car pull up outside and a familiar figure jump out.

Filled as she was with a sudden panic, her hand trembled so much that a lot of the coffee slopped over.

'Steady there.' Noel took the mug from her.

White to the lips, she whispered, 'Oh, dear God, it's Rafe. I don't want to see him. I can't bear it.'

'So don't answer the door.' Noel shrugged.

'He has a key,' she admitted miserably. Then in desperation, 'What am I going to do?'

'I'll soon send him packing... No, better still... Come on, kiddo, let's give the cheating swine an Oscar-winning performance.'

Grabbing her hand, Noel hurried her into the bedroom, coming to a halt in line with the open door.

'Put your arms round my neck and close your eyes,' he instructed. Dropping the towel, he pulled her close and began to kiss her just as the front door opened and Rafe walked in.

Noel broke the kiss, and they both looked towards the man standing there as though the sky had fallen in on him.

Shock, and a kind of raw disbelief, showed in his face,

closely followed by anger. Then the shock and anger iced over
and with a razor-sharp edge to his voice he said, 'So this is
Noel... I can quite see why you didn't want to come to Paris...'

Tossing the key he was holding onto the coffee-table, he
added, 'We'll meet again, Madeleine, one day. Mark my
words...' and, turning on his heel, walked out.

'That's put paid to the swine,' Noel remarked with satisfaction, and, using one hand to cover Madeleine's eyes,
stooped to grab the towel.

'Now, then, if you promise to keep your eyes shut while I
make myself decent, I'll allow you to pour me another mug
of coffee...'

Though she kept them shut, there was no real need to—
they were blinded by tears...

CHAPTER FOUR

As though the fates had conspired against her, the bitter end to the affair coincided with a further blow. After slipping into a deep coma, her mother died three days later at the age of just forty-four.

At the funeral Madeleine was dry-eyed, too frozen for tears. Blaming herself for her mother's death, as she had blamed herself for her husband's, she felt leaden, desolate, weighed down by grief and guilt.

Eve and Noel were the only other mourners. Madeleine's aunt and uncle wrote to offer their condolences, and to apologise for not being there.

The letter ended, 'If you feel like getting right away come and visit with us, do, and stay for as long as you want to.'

The suggestion seemed like a lifeline.

Her job at the clinic was almost over, and Noel, on summer leave, and with nowhere to live, professed himself happy to flat-sit for her.

With Eve's encouragement, Madeleine notified her private patients, and accepted her aunt and uncle's invitation to visit them in Boston.

Her only regret was leaving Katie, who, on hearing the news, threw her thin arms around Madeleine's waist and, her big brown eyes overflowing with tears, cried, 'I don't want you to go.'

'But you're almost better now. If you keep on doing your exercises you don't really need me any longer.'

'I do, I do,' the child wailed.

'I promise I'll come and visit you as soon as I get back, and then you'll be able to show me how well you're managing.'

Tears still running down her cheeks, Katie sniffed dolefully. 'How long will you be gone?'

'I'm not sure,' Madeleine told her. 'A few weeks... A month maybe.'

'I'll miss you, the little girl said, brushing away her tears.'

'Tell you what—suppose I write to you?'

'Can I write back?'

'I'll expect you to. Now, give me a smile, and don't forget to do those exercises.' Madeleine smiled, an ache in her heart as she said goodbye to the little girl who reminded her so much of Rafe.

'I won't.'

When Madeleine arrived in Boston, her aunt and uncle, who had a big house on the edge of the Common, welcomed her with open arms and, seeing how shattered she looked, did their utmost to cheer her up.

For their sakes she tried to appear cheerful, but her mother's death had left her desolate, and she missed Rafe with a raw, ragged, savage pain that made her feel as if she'd been mauled and left for dead.

She had intended to stay in Boston for a month at the most, but, unable to regain her grip, and giving in to her aunt and uncle's urging, the visit lengthened to five weeks.

After six weeks had gone by, feeling unable to accept their generous hospitality any longer, she declared her intention of returning to England.

'Do you *want* to go home?' her aunt asked.

'No,' Madeleine admitted—suppose she ran into Rafe, or saw the announcement of his wedding in the papers?—'but I must get back to work.'

'You're not just worrying about money, are you? We're not exactly poor, and I'm sure—'

'You're very kind, and I appreciate it. But I do want to start work again as soon as possible.'

Agreeing that that might be for the best, her uncle offered her a position in the physical-therapy unit of the Wansdon Heights Fitness Center, which he owned.

After some thought, she accepted. If she stayed safely in Boston, surely sooner or later she would forget about Rafe?

Either that or she was afraid she would grieve for the rest of her life.

Her aunt and uncle were delighted that she was staying and, when she announced her intention of finding a small apartment to rent, urged her to live with them.

'We love having you here, and we've five spare bedrooms. We can turn the biggest into what you Brits call a bedsit.'

She thanked them sincerely but, needing to be independent, insisted on paying a fair rent and keeping herself.

Unable to change her mind, they agreed.

A phone call to London settled that when Noel went back to the Middle East he would hand in the keys to her flat, and Eve would store her relatively few possessions.

That part was easy. The letter to Katie, who was looking forward to having her back, was much harder to write.

The answer came by return. Her parents, apparently to soften the blow, were buying the child a computer for her birthday, and after extracting a promise that Madeleine would keep in touch by email Katie seemed reasonably cheerful.

The fitness centre was extremely busy, and in an effort to put the past behind her and give herself less time to brood

Madeleine chose to work long hours, finding it rewarding and, after a time, therapeutic.

The bleakness of disillusionment, mingled with the longing for what might have been had Rafe proved to be the man of principle she had thought him, began to fade but still never truly left her thoughts. By the time Alan Bannerman joined the staff, she was over the worst. Or so she told herself.

Somehow—perhaps it was his mild manner, his charming diffidence—he got through to her, and when they had been colleagues for some six weeks she accepted a date. A pleasant, undemanding companion, he proved to be an antidote to loneliness.

When they had known each other for three months he asked her to marry him. Thinking him placid and unemotional, she was surprised by how ardently he pressed her. Unable to give him an immediate answer, she asked for time to think it over. She was relieved when he agreed to wait a week, and they arranged to have dinner the following Saturday evening.

When Saturday morning came and Madeleine still hadn't been able to make up her mind, she decided to phone Eve and ask her opinion.

Listening to the familiar voice answer laconically, 'Hello?' she felt a surge of homesickness.

'Hi, it's me.'

'Maddy! It's great to hear from you!' Eve exclaimed. 'How are things?'

'I've got something of a problem.'

'Hang on a minute while I switch off the telly… Right, fire away.'

When Madeleine had told her, Eve exclaimed, 'A man who's not only nice-looking but also decent and dependable wants to marry you and you call *that* a problem?

'Even though the love of my life finally moved in with me six weeks ago, I can't get him to make any sort of commitment, let alone offer to marry me…' Eve moaned. Then quickly added, 'Don't worry, I'm sympathetic really. It must be tough when it's something as important as marriage and you can't make up your mind!'

Madeleine laughed. 'Be serious for a second, Eve; this is important.'

'What's he like in bed?'

'I don't know,' Madeleine admitted.

'So you've been keeping him at arm's length? I can't say I blame you. Once bitten, twice shy… Though if you *do* decide to marry him, it might not be a bad idea to find out what kind of lover he is before you actually say "I will"…'

'That's the problem, Eve,' Madeleine sighed, 'I'm fond of him, but there's no passion.' Then, striving to be fair, 'At least on my side.'

'I thought not. Otherwise you wouldn't still be hesitating. It's Rafe, isn't it? You're still in love with him.'

'No!' Realising her denial had been too vehement, Madeleine added more moderately, 'No, I'm not still in love with him.'

'But you've never really got over him,' Eve concluded.

'It has nothing to do with Rafe.'

Eve grunted her disbelief. 'I think it has everything to do with Rafe.'

'As far as he's concerned it's over and done with. All in the past. Truly.' Madeleine tried to make her voice sound as persuasive as possible.

'Well, I'll believe you, thousands wouldn't. So what do you want me to say?'

'I just want a truthful opinion. Whether or not you think I should go ahead and marry Alan.'

'If you need to ask my opinion, you don't love him enough and you shouldn't be marrying him.'

Put like that it was blindingly simple.

'Thank you,' Madeleine said gratefully.

'Don't thank me until you've made up your mind.'

'It's made up.' Madeleine smiled, relief flooding her voice.

'Atta girl! Is it yes or no?'

'It's no. You're quite right. If I needed to ask your opinion, then I don't love him enough. It wouldn't be fair to marry him. We're having dinner together tonight; I'll tell him then.'

'What will you do when you've told him? I mean, if you work together it could make things difficult.'

Madeleine paused, trying to decide what to do. 'I think, for his sake, I'll have to give in my notice and find another post.'

'I agree. Leave him alone so he can gather up the pieces and get on with his life.'

Madeleine gasped at Eve's bluntness.

'Look on it as being cruel to be kind,' Eve said briskly. 'You'll be doing him no favours by hanging around. Now, how do you feel?'

'I'm not sure. Relieved…a bit sad…restless…unsettled…and just hearing your voice has made me feel dreadfully homesick.'

'You've been there for over a year, Maddy. Why don't you come home?'

All at once, Madeleine very much wanted to. But if she did she would be in the same city as Rafe and run a risk, however small, of seeing him.

And that she couldn't bear.

Just the thought made her skin chill with panic and the fine hairs on the back of her neck rise.

Picking up Madeleine's unspoken fear, Eve brought it into the open. 'Unless you're afraid of running into Rafe?'

'Well, I…'

'London's a big place, Maddy, and it's not as if you normally move in the same social circles.'

'That's true.' Then, saying aloud something she had only thought about, 'He'll no doubt be married to Fiona by now.'

'I guess so. I haven't noticed any mention of it in the papers, but then I don't often get to read the society columns. So how about it? Are you coming home?'

'I'd like to, but...' Madeleine hesitated as the practicalities of the situation struck her. She hadn't managed to save a great deal, and by the time she had paid her airfare she would have very little money left.

'If I come home I won't have a job.' She voiced one of the most serious considerations.

'Presumably you won't have one there when you've left Wansdon Heights, and there are plenty of openings in England for a good physiotherapist.'

'I'd have nowhere to live.' Madeleine sighed.

'Come to me until you find somewhere.'

'You've only got one bedroom.'

'Well, I've a fold-away put-you-up, and I've recently bought a bed-settee, like you used to have, for the lounge.'

Momentarily tempted, then suddenly remembering, Madeleine said hastily, 'I couldn't possibly. What about Dave? He wouldn't want another woman cluttering up the place, even for a short time.'

'He wouldn't dare raise any objections. I'd kick him out if he did.' Eve laughed.

'Please, Eve,' Madeleine cried anxiously, 'don't fall out with him on my account.'

'Hey there, I'm only joking. Where's your sense of humour gone?'

'I'm sorry. I guess I'm just depressed.'

'Then it's high time you pulled yourself together and came back home. You've only been marking time in the States. Why don't you *really* put the past behind you and start living again?'

After a moment, Madeleine said slowly, 'I might just do that,' and started to mean it.

'Honest?' Eve queried.

'Honest.'

'With regard to a job, you could always treat patients privately. Visit them in their own homes, or even take a live-in position, until you find the right kind of opening and accommodation.

'Tell you what, I'm working tomorrow morning, filling in for Tracy. I can check the list of clients who want home-visits and see what new enquiries are coming in. I'll let you know if there's anything that seems suitable... Now, before you go, there's someone here who would like a word with you. Just at the moment he's sleeping on my bed-settee while he looks for a flat.'

'Hi, beautiful!' said a familiar voice.

'Noel!' Madeleine cried, her gladness evident.

'What's my favourite girl been doing?'

'Behaving like an idiot.'

'I don't believe a word of it,' he joked.

'It's great to hear your voice.'

'I thought you'd be pleased. Hurry back, sugar. Seeing me in the flesh is bound to give you an even bigger thrill.'

Laughing, she said, 'I didn't know you were home.'

'I'm back for good, ready to settle down to a nine-to-five job behind a desk.'

Madeleine didn't believe him for a second. 'You're joking, of course.'

'Yes and no. I'm going to give it a try, anyway.'

'Any special reason?' she pried.

'You mean, is there a woman involved? Yes. Her name's Zoe. She's five feet three, with a figure like a dream, short dark hair, and eyes the colour of chocolate. Added to that, she's clever, good-natured and loyal, and she thinks I'm the bee's knees,' he added smugly.

'Well, she would, wouldn't she? You always did have a good sales pitch. Just take care she doesn't discover too many faults,' Madeleine giggled.

'Faults?' He sounded affronted. 'I don't have any faults—like most men, I'm perfect.'

'Of course you are. Sorry.'

'I should think so. However, just in case she hasn't realised all my finer qualities, it wouldn't do any harm to have you on hand to sing my praises…'

'Such as?'

'Well, if you can't think of anything better, you could always tell her how shy and sweet and utterly wonderful I am. If necessary I'll pay you.'

'You want me to lie to her for money?'

He groaned. 'Where are your friends when you need them? Still, I'll forgive you if you come back as soon as possible.'

'I intend to.' Whether or not Eve found anything suitable, Madeleine now knew for certain that she was going home.

'Any chance of making it back for Christmas?'

'I seriously doubt it.'

'There's a cold snap on the way and good odds on it being a white one this year. Remember how, as kids, we used to wish for a white Christmas?'

'I remember,' Madeleine answered wistfully.

'Well, the long-range weather forecast has been for snow nationwide, the mistletoe is up and my lips are pursed ready.'

Madeleine laughed. 'Even with such an incentive, I'm afraid I can't see myself making it until the New Year. But I'll get things moving as fast as possible.'

'You do that. Bye, now. See you soon.'

With a sigh, Madeleine replaced the receiver.

The fact that she was going home would be a blow to her aunt and uncle, and she hated the thought of telling them almost as much as she hated the thought of telling Alan. But it had to be done.

* * *

In the event, telling Alan proved to be an even worse ordeal than she had anticipated. Displaying an unexpected streak of tenacity, he hung on like a terrier, refusing to accept her decision, trying to change her mind.

By the time the uncomfortable meal was over, Madeleine felt totally shattered.

Pleading a headache, which was the truth, she opted for an early night and, fearing a continuation of the pressure, refused his offer to take her home and waved for a cab.

It was obvious that he wasn't going to take no for an answer and, knowing that for both their sakes it would be best to make a quick, clean break, she decided to leave Boston as soon as she could. But as it was only a few days to Christmas, she realized it might prove impossible to get a flight until after the holiday.

As soon as she got back to her bedsit, she called Logan Airport.

Her luck was in.

Due to a last-minute cancellation, there was a seat available on a flight leaving the following evening. Though it was in first class, and she couldn't really afford the extra, she booked it on her credit card.

That done, she breathed a sigh of relief.

When she reached London, she would have just about enough money to enable her to stay in one of the cheaper hotels for a few nights.

How well she managed after that would depend on how soon she could get back to work. If Eve came up with anything suitable…

Thinking of her friend, she reached for the phone. It would be the early hours of the morning in England, so she couldn't tell Eve what she'd done, but she could leave a message.

Having tapped in the familiar number, she waited for the answering machine to cut in, then said, 'Eve, it's Maddy. I've managed to get a seat on a flight leaving Boston tomorrow night. I'll ring tomorrow afternoon, when you're home from work, and give you the details. Bye for now.'

Then, her head throbbing dully, she emailed Katie to tell her the news, before putting on her nightdress and going through to the bathroom to brush her teeth.

She had been sleeping badly lately, but, now she had come to a decision and taken the first positive step towards going home, she should be able to sleep better, she told herself bracingly as she climbed into bed.

For months she had tried not to think about Rafe, but, as though the decision to go back to London had opened the floodgates of memory, she found herself doing just that.

She could see in her mind's eye how his thick, sooty lashes brushed his hard cheeks when he looked down…how his clear green eyes could go silvery with laughter, or dark and smoky with desire…how the creases in his lean cheeks—too male to be called dimples—deepened when he smiled.

She remembered how generous and caring he had been. How willing to give and take, to compromise. Remembered too how masterful and resourceful he could be when he thought it necessary. She had been at the Mayfair clinic one Friday evening when, returning early from what she knew had been a tiring business trip, he'd phoned to suggest that they had dinner together.

Having agreed to work later than usual, and unwilling to keep him hanging about, she had said no, and arranged to meet him the next day for lunch. She had then spent the rest of the evening regretting her decision, and wishing she'd said yes.

When she had left for home, he was waiting for her.

Leaning nonchalantly against his Porsche, wearing casual clothes and, though the sun had gone down, sunglasses, he had straightened at her approach and moved purposefully to bar her way.

Her heart had leapt and gladness fizzed through her like champagne.

'What are you doing here?' As he took her arm and drew her towards the car, she added lightly, 'And why the shades?'

'This is an abduction, doll,' he said in the accent of an American film gangster.

'Good gracious! Didn't I ought to scream?'

'If I was following the script, I should say menacingly, "Not if you know what's good for you".'

'Oh.'

'On the other hand, it would give me an excuse to kiss you,' he drawled laconically.

Lifting her face, she asked demurely, 'Do you need an excuse?'

'An invitation's better. Not that I really need either.' Bending his dark head, he kissed her with a hungry passion that showed how much he'd missed her.

Then, as though his lips couldn't bring themselves to part from hers, he murmured between soft, baby kisses, 'I can't wait to make love to you. I've thought about nothing else while I've been away.

'This afternoon, in Paris, I brought an important board-meeting to an early close because I couldn't concentrate. I kept imagining I was undressing you, touching you, feeling your response... I couldn't wait to get back, to make it all happen...'

A little breathlessly, she asked, 'So what are we doing standing here?'

'That's a good question.'

He hurried her into the car and, sliding in beside her, started the engine.

When they turned down an unfamiliar road, she queried, 'Where are we going?'

Sounding happy and carefree, he told her, 'To a little inn

called the Woolpack. It's right off the beaten track and no one will care if we stay in bed for the entire weekend.'

'Oh, but I…'

He glanced at her sharply. 'I hope you're not going to tell me you have other commitments?'

Judging from his tone, if she said yes it would precipitate a showdown, and she wasn't prepared.

Brushing guilt aside, she decided that just for once she could miss her usual weekend visits to the nursing home.

Never easy at telling lies, she swallowed and said, 'I was going to say I haven't got a toothbrush or any clean undies.'

She felt him relax.

'That's all been taken care of,' he told her. 'I paid a visit to your flat and picked up what I thought you might need.'

Giving her a wicked sidelong glance, he added, 'I didn't bother to pack a nightie.'

The carefree mood was back, and with a little sigh, she rested her head lightly against his arm for a moment. 'I've missed you.'

He gave her knee a brief squeeze. 'Next time I have to go to Paris I'd like you with me.'

By the time they arrived at the Woolpack, a blue dusk was spreading gauzy veils over the countryside and bats were flittering about.

The lamplit inn, a lopsided, half-timbered black and white building with overhanging eaves and tall, crooked chimneys, looked as if it belonged in some Charles Dickens novel.

They were greeted by a plump and smiling landlady who showed them up to a small room under the eaves with a tiny *en suite* bathroom and black oak floorboards that creaked at every step.

The ceiling sloped steeply, and the low casement windows were thrown open to the balmy night air. A high, old-fashioned double bed, with a goose-feather mattress and sheets that smelled of lavender, took up most of the space.

A tray with a bottle of champagne and a plate of hors d'oeuvres was waiting by the bedside.

When they had thanked the landlady she wished them a cheerful, 'Goodnight,' and bustled away.

Rafe dropped their bags on a low chest and helped Madeleine out of her light jacket, before shedding his own. Then, glancing at the tray, he queried, 'Hungry?'

'Yes. But not for food.'

He gave a low growl and, sweeping her into his arms, carried her over to the bed.

Even though his need was every bit as urgent as hers, he didn't hurry as he stripped off first her clothes and then his own and joined her.

Her arms went round his neck while his hands shaped and moulded her, clasping her hips to pull her firmly against his lower body, before making love to her with an unleashed passion that sent her up in flames.

When the heated rapture settled into a contented glow they lay in bed, kissing occasionally and feeding each other delicacies between sips of champagne.

It was lovely and romantic, and Madeleine had never been happier.

Afterwards, as though they couldn't get enough of one another, they had made love again, and again, and, reliving that night, all the pleasure and warmth, she found herself trapped in a sensual haze.

Only when the haze cleared and she realised she was alone was the warmth replaced by such bleak desolation that she felt like crying.

Though what good would crying do? It was over. All in the past. She must forget Rafe. Forget the way he had made her feel. Forget the happiness he had brought her. Dismiss him from her thoughts and not look back.

But that was easier said than done.

After a restless night spent tossing and turning, she woke next morning heavy-eyed and unrefreshed, still feeling cold inside.

Jumping out of bed, she headed for the bathroom. But, while a hot shower heated her skin, it failed to cure that inner chill of loss.

When her aunt and uncle returned from church and asked her to join them for lunch, she broke the news that she had refused Alan's proposal and was returning to England.

Though they were sorry to lose her, they accepted her decision without attempting to change her mind… Grateful to them both, she kissed them and thanked them sincerely for all they'd done.

Then, after writing and posting a short, difficult letter to Alan, she tidied her room and packed her few belongings.

Her cases zipped and ready, she made herself a pot of tea and was just reaching for the phone to call Eve, when it rang, making her jump.

Wondering if it might be Alan, she answered cautiously, 'Hello?'

'Maddy?'

'Eve! I was just going to ring you. I presume you got the message I left?'

'Yes, I did. Now, that's what I call getting a move-on. How did Alan react when you told him you couldn't marry him? You have told him, I presume?'

'Yes, I told him last night. He refused to take no for an answer.' Madeleine sighed.

'In that case you're doing the right thing. You need to get

out of there as quickly as possible for both your sakes. How did your aunt and uncle take it?'

'Better than I'd expected. They're disappointed, of course, but they didn't try to put pressure on me.'

'Thank the lord for small mercies. Now for my news. As soon as I got to the clinic I checked through the requests for physiotherapy. There was nothing that seemed up your street. Quite disappointing really.

'Then just before I was due to go home I had a phone call from a Mrs Rampling, who desperately needs help. Her husband had a stroke some three months ago, and at the same time fractured his hip. She's worried that he's making very little progress. It seems he's a difficult man who hates hospitals and clinics, but he's agreed to have a physiotherapist treat him at home.

'She told me that what she really needs is someone who would be willing to live in for as long as it takes to give him a better quality of life.'

'Where do the Ramplings live?'

'I gather that at the moment they're living in Kent, in a big house near the village of Hethersage.

'Apart from the fact that Mr Rampling can be 'uncooperative', I must say that it sounds like a good bet. The salary she mentioned is generous in the extreme, and you'd have your own self-contained accommodation. Interested?'

Without hesitation, Madeleine said, 'Very.'

'Then perhaps you should give her a ring? If you can find a pen and paper, here's the number...'

When Madeleine rang the number Eve had given her, a woman's pleasant voice repeated the number, then added, 'Harriet Rampling speaking.'

'Mrs Rampling, it's Madeleine Knight.'

'Oh, Miss Knight... How good of you to ring me so promptly. I gather from Miss Collins that you're still in the States?'

'That's right.'

'If the salary I suggested is acceptable, would you be willing to come to us on your return? For a trial period at least?'

'Yes, certainly,' Madeleine answered eagerly.

'Oh, that is good news!'

'I understand you live in Kent, near Hethersage?'

'Yes, we've been living there since my husband came out of hospital. Normally we live in London, but we're having our house at Regent's Park extensively altered, to make life easier for George. Until it's finished, which looks like being several more weeks, our son suggested we stay with him at Hethersage Hall.

'It is a good-sized place and we have our own ground-floor accommodation. There's also a comfortable self-contained flat we hoped might be suitable for you. It's not huge, but it does have a reasonable living room, a bedroom, a kitchen and an outside stairway which gives some degree of privacy.'

Then a shade anxiously, 'I think you'll like it.'

'I'm sure I will,' Madeleine concluded.

She heard a distinct sigh of relief before Mrs Rampling went on, 'You can either eat with us or do your own thing, whichever suits you. I gather you're returning to England quite soon?'

'I'm leaving Boston tonight. I should be arriving in London tomorrow morning.'

'Do you have any immediate plans? Anyone you want to spend Christmas with before you come to us?'

While Madeleine knew that Eve would make her welcome, she also knew there was very little room in the small flat. And now Dave had moved in, and Noel was sleeping there, it would be quite impossible.

Added to that, Eve and Dave and Noel and Zoe made a foursome. *She* would be the odd one out. It wasn't a situation she fancied. 'No, not really.'

'You have no family?'

'No. My mother died just over a year ago, and my father's in California. I shall probably book into a hotel until after the holiday.'

'Perhaps you *want* to stay in London…?'

'Not particularly,' Madeleine added.

'Then wouldn't it make more sense to come straight to the hall?'

Tempted, Madeleine hesitated. The thought of spending the holiday alone in a hotel wasn't particularly appealing, and, now that she'd splurged on a first-class ticket, money was even tighter than she had anticipated.

'Well, I…I wouldn't want to intrude on your family over Christmas.'

'My dear, of course you wouldn't be intruding… Though, as a matter of fact, George and I are flying up to Scotland first thing tomorrow morning. We're staying with our son and daughter over Christmas and the New Year.' Her excitement evident, she added, 'They have a brand-new baby boy, and both George and I are looking forward immensely to seeing our latest grandson.'

Then, getting back to practicalities, 'Our being away from the hall will give you breathing space, and also a good chance to settle into your flat. What do you say?'

It would be ideal in some ways, Madeleine thought, though it would leave her with Mrs Rampling's other son and his family. Unless they too were going away?

But even if they weren't, she needn't feel she was intruding. The flat was self-contained, so she could keep herself to herself.

'In that case I'll be happy to, if you're sure that arrangement suits you, and your son won't mind?'

'Quite sure. That's all settled, then.

'Mary Boyce, the housekeeper, will have everything ready for you, and if you can tell me your flight number and what time you're due to land, we'll send Jack, Mary's husband, to pick you up.'

'Thank you.' Madeleine gave her the information.

Sounding warm and friendly, Mrs Rampling added, 'Do make yourself at home. Though it will be January before we actually meet, I'm looking forward to it. Have a good flight.'

'Goodbye, and thank you again.'

Relieved and excited, Madeleine quickly called Eve to give her the good news and thank her.

'What are friends for?' she asked. Then, with more than a hint of uncertainty, 'But are you sure you want to give this a shot? After all, you don't really know what you'll be letting yourself in for.'

'Hey, everything's arranged. Don't try and talk me out of it now. It's much too late.'

Then curiously, 'You seemed to be all in favour earlier. Why have you changed your mind?'

'At the time I was quite convinced it was in your best interests, but now I…I can't help having second thoughts.'

'Don't worry, I'm sure everything will be fine.'

Still sounding anxious, unlike herself, Eve said, 'I just hope everything turns out all right. But if it doesn't work, you can always come to us, you know. We'll manage somehow.'

'Thanks,' Madeleine said gratefully.

'Now, don't forget, if you're not happy with the situation, let me know straight away.'

CHAPTER FIVE

AFTER a technical fault that made the big jet almost two hours late getting airborne, the flight was smooth and uneventful.

Madeleine could never sleep on planes, and after so many disturbed nights she was feeling shattered by the time they landed.

The formalities over, she changed her dollars into pounds and, bearing in mind the warnings she had received, slipped half the money into her handbag and the other half into her flight bag.

Both bags on her shoulder, she was heading for the exit when a uniformed chauffeur approached her and queried, 'Miss Knight?'

Wondering how he had managed to pick her out of such a crowd, she answered, 'Yes, that's right.'

'Mrs Rampling asked me to meet you.'

'I'm sorry you've had to wait so long.'

'That's all right, miss,' he said politely. 'When I discovered the flight was running late I used the time to get some breakfast. Now, if you'll come with me, miss, the car's waiting outside.'

She willingly surrendered the unwieldy baggage trolley and followed his short, thick-set figure out to a sleek grey limousine.

It was a bitterly cold, curiously still day, with a sky that gleamed grey and pearly, as iridescent as the inside of a mussel shell.

After the warmth of the terminal, Madeleine found herself starting to shiver in the bleak air. But with a speed and efficiency she could only admire she was installed in the luxurious car, and her luggage stowed away.

The comfortable seats were covered in soft fawn leather and it was pleasantly warm. Almost before they were clear of the airport, lack of sleep catching up on her, her eyelids began to droop and she slipped into a doze.

When she surfaced they were travelling along a quiet country road with skeletal trees on one side and an old lichen-covered wall on the other.

Stifling a yawn, she sat up straighter and looked around her just as they reached a stone-built gatehouse with tall, barley-sugar chimneys and mullioned windows.

As they turned towards the entrance, a pair of black ornamental gates slid aside at their approach and closed behind them.

Rolling parkland stretched away on either side as they followed a serpentine drive that ran between high, mossy banks.

Hethersage Hall, hidden from sight until they had rounded the final bend, was wrapped snugly in a fold in the hills. It was a homely, rambling place, not at all stiff and starchy as its name suggested.

The walls were mellow stone, the roofs a natural slate. Half a dozen gables peaked and sloped at various odd angles, yet the whole thing had a charming symmetry. There were diamond-leaded windows and an oak front door that was metal-studded and silvery with age.

When the car drew to a halt on the cobbled apron and the chauffeur helped Madeleine out, the door was opened wide and a small, plump woman with curly grey hair appeared, smiling a greeting.

'Miss Knight… I'm Mary Boyce, the housekeeper… Do come in out of the cold…'

Returning her smile, Madeleine followed her into a large

wood-panelled hall with polished oak floorboards and dark antique furniture that glowed with the patina of age.

The huge fireplace was full of pine logs, and above the stone mantel there were green spruce boughs and spectacular swags of ivy and scarlet-berried holly. A bunch of mistletoe hung from a fine old chandelier, and a tall, beautifully decorated Christmas tree filled one corner.

Cheerful and garrulous, Mrs Boyce went on, 'You must be weary. Goodness knows jet lag's bad enough, but when there's a long delay on top of that…!'

'Mr and Mrs Rampling send their sincere apologies that they weren't able to greet you in person. They've gone to Scotland to spend the holiday with their son and daughter and their family.'

'Yes, Mrs Rampling did explain.'

'Well, now, if you'd like to come through to the living room…'

The living room was white-walled and spacious, with oak beams and casement windows that looked over a pleasant garden.

It was furnished with an eclectic mix of old and new— some beautiful antiques, a modern suite upholstered in soft natural leather, an Oriental carpet that made Madeleine catch her breath, and several paintings by Jonathan Cass. The sight of which gave her a pang. Rafe had owned several of Cass's snow scenes.

When she was ensconced in a deep armchair in front of a blazing log fire, Mrs Boyce said, 'I'll get you something to eat while Jack takes your luggage up.'

Feeling too tired to eat, Madeleine said, 'Thanks, but I'm not at all hungry. Though a cup of tea would be lovely.'

'Then a cup of tea it is.'

By the time she came back with a tray of tea and homemade cake, made even more soporific by the warmth of the fire, Madeleine was having a serious struggle to stay awake.

Watching her stifle a yawn, Mrs Boyce put the tray down on a small oval table and, proceeding to pour the tea, said sympathetically, 'You must be more than ready to get some sleep.'

'I am tired,' Madeleine admitted.

'Well, as soon as you've finished your tea you can get your head down.' Adding, 'I'll be back in a few minutes to show you round the flat,' the housekeeper bustled away.

Madeleine was just finishing her second cup of tea when Mrs Boyce returned and queried, 'If you're ready?' Then, in concern, 'I'm not rushing you, am I?'

'No, not at all, I'm quite ready.'

As she followed the housekeeper across the hall and up a graceful curving staircase with a griffin head as its newel post, she looked around her.

It was a beautiful old house, she thought, utterly charming and unpretentious, with its simple white walls and black beams, its polished oak floorboards and linenfold panelling.

At the top of the stairs Mrs Boyce turned left down a short, wide corridor, and opened a door at the end.

'Here we are.'

The living room was warm and cosy with an old, gently faded rose-pink carpet, matching curtains and a comfortable-looking suite. On the mantel was a small chiming clock.

Though there was discreet central heating, a log fire burnt in a delightful little fireplace with a tiled surround and an elaborately carved fender. To one side, a basket was filled with pine logs and cones that gave off an aromatic scent.

'What a lovely room!' Madeleine exclaimed.

Mrs Boyce looked worried. 'There's just one thing; I discovered earlier that the phone up here isn't working. I really don't know what's wrong with it.

'Of course, you could always use one of the downstairs phones.'

'That won't be necessary,' Madeleine assured her. 'I have a mobile.'

Looking pleased that the problem had been solved so easily, the housekeeper led the way into a pretty, feminine bedroom with an *en suite* bathroom.

Having turned back the duvet on the double bed, she indicated the cases which had been placed on an oak linen chest next to a cheval-glass. 'If you want any help with your unpacking, I'm sure Annie will give you a hand…

'And this is the kitchen…'

Madeleine glanced around the well-equipped kitchen, which was bright and airy, with a natural pine table and chairs, primrose tiles and muslin curtains at the casement windows.

'I hope it meets with your approval?'

'It certainly does,' Madeleine assured her. 'The whole flat is really lovely.'

The housekeeper beamed. 'Mrs Rampling will be pleased. She was anxious that you should like it.

'Now, you'll find plenty of food in the fridge and cupboards,' she opened the relevant doors to prove it, 'but if there's anything else you want, Annie will no doubt be shopping in the morning. She's taking over the household duties until after the Christmas holiday.

'There, now,' she said as, the short tour over, they went back to the living room, 'I'll leave you to get some sleep.'

At the door she turned. 'Oh, I almost forgot; as it's your first night here, the master is hoping you'll join him for an evening meal…'

There had been no mention made of either a wife or a family, Madeleine realised, though presumably there was a Mrs Rampling junior.

She was just about to ask, when the housekeeper added,

'Pre-dinner drinks are served at seven in the study, which is directly across the hall from the bottom of the stairs.'

A second later she had closed the door behind her and departed.

Though the invitation to dinner had been carefully phrased, it held an underlying hint of command that for some reason Madeleine found vaguely disturbing.

She was a free agent, Mrs Rampling had made that clear, and if 'the master' had any ideas to the contrary… Well, he wasn't employing her, she reminded herself, and, if the worst came to the worst, she could always leave.

Irritated with herself, she sighed. She'd only just got here. Why was she thinking of leaving before she'd even met the man?

It wasn't like her.

Deciding that it was simply because she was so tired, she pushed her irritability aside and glanced around the living room once more.

On the far wall, a door with irregular panels of old glass gave access to an outside stone stairway guarded by a wrought-iron rail.

The doors to the bedroom and kitchen were plain oak, while the door to the main part of the house was handsomely carved. As she admired it she noticed there was no key in the ornate lock, and felt a faint stirring of unease.

Be sensible, she scolded herself; as the flat was part of the house, there should be no need to lock the door. Yet still that slight feeling of unease persisted, refusing to be banished.

A closer inspection showed that, though the door leading to the stone stairway was securely locked and bolted, neither it, nor any of the internal doors, boasted a key. Not even the bathroom.

But if the lack of keys became a problem she could always talk to Mrs Boyce about it, she decided as she went through to the bedroom.

Much too weary to do all her unpacking, she dug out a change of clothing for the evening, her night things, her sponge bag, her cosmetic purse and her alarm clock.

As she stripped off her clothes and donned her nightdress she saw with delight that it had started to snow, big flakes that drifted down like feathers from an angel's wing.

From being a child, she had always loved snow, and for a short time she watched the magical sight before closing the curtains.

To make certain she didn't sleep too long, she set the alarm for six-thirty, then climbed thankfully into bed.

Madeleine had been asleep for some time when she began to dream. She heard a noise in the outer room, the faint click of a latch as a door was opened and closed quietly. That was followed by the stealthy brush of footsteps crossing a carpet, and in the way that dreamers did she knew that something menacing was standing just outside her bedroom door.

She got out of bed, but couldn't bring herself to open the door and confront whoever or whatever stood there. Instead, she went through a door on the far wall and found herself in a dark, narrow corridor. Almost immediately she heard the footsteps behind her and fear clutched at her heart…

She began to run blindly, down endless pitch-black corridors, the thing at her heels getting closer…gaining on her… She could hear whatever it was breathing now…

Abruptly the corridor came to a dead end. She was feeling frantically for a door, or some other way out, when a cold hand reached out of the darkness to touch her…

With a half-stifled scream she woke up, shuddering and panting, her heart thudding against her ribcage.

As consciousness kicked in the nightmare faded, and just briefly she was disorientated until she remembered where she was.

Reaching for the light switch, she flooded the room with light, blinking a little as her eyes adjusted to the brightness.

A glance at the clock showed it was just turned six. Thankfully she realised that there was ample time to shower and change before she had to go down to dinner.

She would have much preferred to stay in the flat and have a snack in front of the living-room fire rather than dining with the family, but as she would be living in their house it would make sense to start off on the right foot.

In spite of the abrupt awakening she felt rested and refreshed, and, turning off the alarm, she stretched luxuriously before climbing out of bed and heading for the bathroom.

Through the frosted glass she could make out that everywhere was covered with a white blanket and it was still snowing heavily. It looked as though Noel had been right when he'd forecast a white Christmas.

By half-past six she was showered and dressed in a simple dinner dress in a silky grey material, her make-up in place and her blonde hair taken up into a gleaming coil.

Intending to make a quick phone call to Eve, she went through to the living room, which was still comfortably warm though the fire had burnt out, and looked around for her handbag.

Her flight bag was there but not her handbag. Where on earth had she put it?

A brief search revealed no sign of it. Neither did a more thorough one.

She could almost have sworn that she'd brought both bags up, but she'd been so dazed with tiredness, she couldn't be absolutely sure.

Had she left it in the car?

No, she thought with certainty, she could definitely remember having the two bags with her in the living room. She had put them down between the side of the chair and the coffee-table, so she must have only picked up her flight bag and left her handbag behind.

But there was plenty of time to fetch it and still have a word with Eve before dinner.

Everywhere was still and silent, not a soul in sight, as she descended the stairs. Through the diamond-leaded panes of the landing window she could see that the snow was coming down even faster and a rising wind was whipping it along.

As she crossed the hall she paused for a moment to admire the Christmas tree with its gleaming star on top and all its candlelights glowing. For anyone to have gone to so much trouble, there must be children in the house.

Unwilling to burst in on the family unexpectedly, when she reached the living room she knocked.

There was no answer, and she opened the door to find that the room was deserted. Crossing to the chair she'd sat in earlier that day, she bent to pick up her bag.

It was no longer there.

For a moment she was nonplussed.

But of course the housekeeper must have found it and, unwilling to disturb her, taken charge of it.

Oh, well, she thought philosophically, she could always ring Eve after dinner.

When she reached the study she found that too was deserted. It was a comfortable, homely room. Built-in bookcases flanked the fireplace, and in the corner a grandfather clock ticked sonorously. Next to it, an octagonal table held a phone and a silver-framed photograph of a gentle-faced woman with greying hair.

Several standard lamps cast pools of golden light, and a log fire blazed and crackled on the wide stone hearth. Below the mantel were bright garlands of holly and mistletoe and ivy.

On the far left, through a partly open door, Madeleine

glimpsed an adjoining office with an imposing desk that held a computer and an array of state-of-the-art equipment.

She glanced at the clock and, finding it was still only ten minutes to seven, sat down in one of the deep leather armchairs drawn up to the fire.

As she gazed into the flames, her thoughts went back to an old pub near Rye that Rafe had taken her to more than a year ago. It had been a chilly September day and they had lunched in front of a blazing fire.

She could see his face with the firelight flickering on it. Visualise the tiny crescent-shaped scar at the corner of his mouth, the way he tilted his head, the quick, sidelong smile, the tough male beauty that never failed to make her heart beat faster...

Though she hadn't heard anyone come in, some instinct made her lift her head and look up.

A tall, dark-haired man stood only a couple of feet away, his eyes fixed on her face.

Shock hit her in the chest like a clenched fist.

But it couldn't be Rafe. It *couldn't*.

Convinced she was seeing things, she squeezed her eyes shut.

When she opened them again he was still standing there, his green eyes cool, his face shuttered, silently watching her.

Her heart began to pound like a trip-hammer, her head went dizzy and the blood roared in her ears, while darkness swooped, threatening to engulf her and drag her down into the depths.

Somehow she fought against it and won.

But still she could neither move nor speak, and for what seemed an age she simply sat and gaped at him.

Wearing charcoal-grey trousers and a fine black sweater that pulled taut across his wide shoulders, he looked both disturbing and dangerous.

He was the first to break the silence. 'You're even lovelier than I remember.' His tone was as cool and biting as his gaze, so that the remark sounded more like condemnation than a compliment.

'Why are you here?' Her voice shook so badly that the words were barely intelligible.

He smiled thinly. 'This is my house.'

She made a movement of denial. 'Mrs Rampling said her son owned Hethersage Hall.'

'I'm Harriet's son. Or, rather, her godson.'

'I don't understand,' Madeleine said jerkily. 'I thought your godparents were called Charn…'

'Yes, they were. However, when Harriet had been a widow for almost two years, she met and married George Rampling, a middle-aged widower with three grown-up children and a couple of grandchildren…'

But Madeleine was no longer listening. Her thoughts skittering about like mad things, she realised that, as Rafe and Fiona must be married by now, *this* was Fiona's house.

Oh, dear God. She might walk in at any minute! Panic-stricken at the thought, Madeleine jumped to her feet. She must get away.

She had only taken a couple of steps when Rafe's fingers closed around her wrist like a steel manacle.

'Don't rush off.'

'Please let me go…' For a moment or two she tried to pull free.

When, finding it was useless, she stopped he loosened his grip a little and, leading her back to the chair, pressed her into it.

'I want to leave,' she whispered.

He shook his head. 'Harriet was so pleased you were coming, so you really must stay. Otherwise I'll get the blame for driving you away.'

'What about your wife?' Madeleine blurted out.

He raised dark brows.

'*She* won't want me here.'

'What makes you think that?' he asked interestedly.

For a moment she almost admitted the truth, then better sense prevailed and she began carefully, 'As Mrs Rampling isn't here and your wife *is*—'

Once again he shook his head. 'She isn't.'

For a moment all Madeleine could feel was relief that Fiona wouldn't walk in and find her there.

'But I'm neglecting my duties as a host,' Rafe went on smoothly. 'What can I get you to drink?'

'I don't want anything to drink, thank you.' Then, more firmly, 'I've no intention of staying. I'm going back to London. Now.'

'I'm afraid I can't ask Jack to turn out again on a night like this.'

'I'll phone for a taxi.'

'And do you think you'll get one?'

'Surely the conditions can't be that bad?' she protested hoarsely.

'When I came home some time ago it was all I could do to get up the drive, and it's been blowing a blizzard ever since.'

She lifted her chin. 'If necessary I'll walk down to the main road and wait for it there.'

'Do you know how long the drive is?'

'No,' she admitted.

He smiled mirthlessly. 'I thought not. It's the best part of a mile, and because it's in a dip the snow is collecting there. And even if you *could* struggle to the end of the drive, in weather like this I doubt if they've managed to keep even the main road open. In any event, you haven't a hope in hell of getting a taxi, so you may as well sit down and relax.'

'I'd prefer to go back up to the flat.' She got to her feet and started for the door on trembling legs.

Rafe easily reached it first and stood with his back to the panels, barring her way. 'And I'd much prefer you to stay here.'

She wanted desperately to push past him, but he looked so tall and dark and menacing that she hadn't the nerve to try.

When she hesitated, he added silkily, 'I've been looking forward to having a talk with you.'

'Then you already knew it was me your godmother had engaged?'

'Oh, yes. When Harriet mentioned your name I was able to tell her I knew you, that you'd been Katie's physiotherapist. She could hardly believe her luck.

'I would have been at the airport to meet you, but I didn't want you to change your mind about coming to Hethersage.'

Firmly, she said, 'Well, I've no intention of staying. If I can't go tonight, I'll leave first thing in the morning.'

He smiled a little. 'We'll see, shall we? In the meanwhile, suppose we sit down and talk?'

'We've nothing to talk about.'

'That's just where you're wrong.' Cupping her elbow, he led her back to the chair and waited for her to sit before moving to the drinks trolley.

Just briefly, Madeleine debated making a run for it, but common sense told her she would be wasting her time. He would catch her before she even reached the flat, and if she *did* manage to get there first she wouldn't be able to lock him out.

Turning to look at her, he queried, 'So what's it to be?'

'I've already told you I don't want a drink.'

Ignoring her churlishness, he filled a glass with a pale Amontillado and offered it to her, his green eyes daring her to refuse.

Weakly, she took it.

Pouring himself a whisky, he sat down opposite and regarded her. He looked eminently satisfied, she decided resentfully, well-aware that he was the master of the situation. Well-aware that she knew it.

From being a life-saver, she thought bleakly, this offer of a job had turned into a nightmare. Sipping the unwanted sherry, she stared into the flames, trying to sort out the confusion in her mind. Surely being offered a post in Rafe's house was too much of a coincidence?

Yet it couldn't have been planned... Or could it?

But if it *had* been planned, why? What could Rafe possibly hope to gain?

The answer was, he had nothing to gain and everything to lose if Fiona found out.

But still the suspicion was there, and Madeleine wondered, had Rafe, for whatever reason, put his godmother up to it? Had George Rampling really any need for a physiotherapist, or had the whole thing been an elaborate hoax?

Though how could they possibly have known she was coming back to England? It had been such a last-minute decision that no one other than Eve and Noel had known.

Except Katie.

She had emailed the child late on Saturday night, so it would have been the following morning before she read it, and later on that same day Mrs Rampling had contacted Grizedale Clinic...

But how had she known to do that? How *could* she have known...?

'Penny for your thoughts.' Rafe's voice sounded amused, a little mocking.

Madeleine looked up slowly and met those gleaming eyes. 'Does Mr Rampling really need physiotherapy, or was the whole thing just a pack of lies?'

'No, everything that Harriet told you was true. She's been on the lookout for a live-in physiotherapist for weeks now.'

'So are you saying that my being here is nothing but a coincidence?'

Rafe raised an eyebrow mockingly. 'Would you believe that?'

'No,' she replied sternly.

He smiled briefly. 'I wouldn't have expected you to. As a matter of fact it was carefully planned.'

Fear sidled up to her and took her hand. With a sickening feeling that she'd walked into some kind of a trap, she felt her mouth go dry and the blood in her veins turn to ice.

Putting the sherry glass on the table with shaking fingers, she crossed her arms and rubbed her palms up and down her bare arms as though she was cold.

The last time they had met, he'd said, '*One day we'll meet again…*' That was all. He hadn't said what he would do when they did meet, but there had been an underlying threat in the quietly spoken words, a hint of menace, that even now made her shiver at the memory.

Making an effort to fight off the panic, she told herself stoutly that she was just being silly. What could he possibly do to her?

But there was a hardness about him, a barely leashed anger, that made her afraid.

Unsteadily, she demanded, 'How did you know I was coming home?'

'How do you think?'

'Katie?'

'Got it in one. Knowing I was—shall we say?—*interested*, Diane has been keeping me up-to-date on what was happening in Boston. When she got your email, Katie was so excited she couldn't wait to tell her mother.' The ice clinked in his whisky glass as he took a sip.

'That still doesn't explain how you found out enough to be able to trick me into coming here. How you knew I was looking for a live-in post. Only Eve…' She stopped speaking abruptly.

Remembering their last conversation, her friend's strange volte-face, her obvious uneasiness, the way she had admitted to having second thoughts, Madeleine asked sharply, 'When did you talk to Eve?'

'When Diane told me you were coming home I wanted to know exactly what your plans were, and I felt sure Eve would know. I finally managed to contact her at the clinic, and after some initial resistance on her part we had quite a long talk. She told me what she was trying to do for you, and I mentioned I might be able to help.

'All I had to do was suggest to Harriet that she rang the clinic's physiotherapy department and talked to a Miss Collins—which she was only too pleased to do.'

So as well as using his godmother, he had used Eve… But what had he said to her to get her to talk to him? And why hadn't Eve told *her*?

As if she'd spoken the thought aloud, he said, 'In the end it was easier than I'd anticipated. I didn't even need to ask Eve not to say anything. It was she who suggested that it would be better if you didn't know I was involved until we'd had a chance to talk. I think she was afraid you might change your mind about coming back…'

There was a tap at the door, and the housekeeper put her head round to say, 'Dinner's all ready when you are.'

'Thank you, Mary, we'll serve ourselves. You can leave anything else that needs to be done until Annie gets here.'

'Thanks… I'll say goodnight, then.'

'Goodnight.'

As the latch clicked, realising belatedly that she should have used the opportunity to escape, Madeleine jumped to her feet and started for the door, crying, 'Mrs Boyce—'

An arm snaked round her waist and a cool hand covered her mouth.

Pulling her back against him, Rafe put his lips to the side of her neck and murmured softly, 'That's not on, my sweet. I don't want Mary involved.'

Trembling, shaken to the core by the caress that was no caress, she stood quite still.

As soon as he released her, she rounded on him. 'And I don't want to be kept here against my will.'

Then, helplessly, 'I can't understand what you're hoping to gain, why you went to so much trouble to get me here.'

He took a stray tendril of blonde hair that had escaped and tugged it gently, making her flinch away. 'It was no trouble. In fact the whole thing worked incredibly smoothly.'

She gritted her teeth. 'Why—?'

'We'll talk about it after dinner.'

'I don't want any dinner.'

His green, lazy-river eyes heavy-lidded and sensual, he said, 'Well, if you really don't want to eat, I can think of something a great deal more exciting to do...'

Wondering frantically if he meant what she thought he meant, she stared up at him.

Softly, he went on, 'So it will suit me fine if you decide against eating.'

He held out both hands. 'Shall we go upstairs?'

CHAPTER SIX

HER normally low, well-modulated voice shrill, she cried, 'No, I don't want you to touch me. I couldn't bear it.'

'The choice is yours.' He smiled. Seeing her expression change, he sighed. 'I gather eating's preferable.'

'*Anything* would be preferable,' she said primly.

'Sassy, eh?' Taking her chin, he tilted her face up to his.

Every nerve ending in her body jerked, and it was all she could do to keep from crying out.

Watching what little colour she had drain away, he remarked silkily, 'I'm beginning to think you're scared of me.'

'Well, you're wrong,' she retorted.

'You mean you're not?'

'No, I'm not,' she lied. 'I just can't bear you to touch me.'

'So you said. But I'm afraid you're going to have to get used to it…'

The faint hum and beep of a fax machine cut through his words.

'If you'll excuse me for just a moment, I'll make sure that's nothing important.' He disappeared into the office.

Her legs feeling too weak to support her, she sank down in the nearest chair. As she did so her eyes lit on the phone on the nearby table. Eve had said, 'Now, don't forget, if you're not happy with the situation, let me know straight away.'

If she could put Eve in the picture, it would seem like a lifeline. With a nervous glance towards the office, she hurried across and picked up the receiver.

She was just tapping in the number when a lean, tanned hand reached over her shoulder and depressed the receiver rest. As she caught her breath, he took the receiver from her hand and replaced it.

'Dear me,' he said mildly. 'It seems I can't take my eyes off you.'

Turning to face him in the confined space, she said as steadily as possible, 'I promised to ring Eve…'

He studied her face, and she tingled under the scrutiny of those green eyes. 'There'll be time for that later.'

'I'd prefer to do it now,' she insisted.

'Our meal will be spoiling…' He reached out a lazy hand and stroked a fingertip down her cheek. Her body trapped between his and the table, she stood perfectly still, afraid to move.

'Unless you've changed your mind about eating?' he queried.

'No, I haven't changed my mind,' she said thickly.

He sighed. 'A pity, but still…'

One hand cupping her bare elbow, he led her to the white-walled, black-beamed dining room, where a candlelit refectory table was set for two.

Several huge logs blazed cheerfully in a Crusader grate, and over the mantel were more garlands of holly and ivy and mistletoe threaded through with gleaming scarlet ribbon.

A thick sheepskin rug lay in front of the stone hearth, and a couch was drawn up before the blaze. Waiting on the coffee-table was a tray with cups and saucers, cream and sugar.

When Madeleine was seated at the table Rafe turned to a massive sideboard, where on a hotplate a glass jug of coffee was bubbling away next to an array of silver dishes.

Removing the covers, he began to fill two plates with roast chicken and vegetables. Then, setting one of them in front of her, he sat down opposite, poured the Chablis and waited pointedly until she picked up her fork and began to eat.

His remark about her having to get used to his touch had sounded very much like a threat and, afraid to ask, she wondered nervously just what he'd meant by it.

'Worried that you'll end up in my bed?' His voice was laced with intent.

Glancing up, she answered with spirit, 'Not when you have a wife.'

'I don't have a wife.'

Wits scattered, she stammered, 'Y-you said your wife wasn't here.'

'Well, as I haven't got one, she wouldn't be, would she?' he countered reasonably.

'You're not married?' She could hardly believe it.

'No, I'm not married,' he said patiently.

'But I thought…'

'What did you think?'

For a second or two she floundered, then, gathering herself, said, 'That with a house like this you'd be married and starting a family.'

'It isn't mandatory,' he responded drily.

'Neither is ending up in your bed.'

He saluted her spirit. 'But you will.'

'Is that misplaced confidence, or merely conceit?'

'Try fate.' He laughed.

Teeth clenched on her bottom lip, she returned her attention to her plate.

Rafe said nothing further, and for a while only the sound of the wind roaring in the chimney and the mellow tick-tock of the casement clock in the corner broke the silence.

While she made a pretence of eating, Madeleine's thoughts

tumbled about like ringside clowns. Why wasn't he married after more than a year? Fiona had made it sound as if the wedding was practically a *fait accompli*.

Was he still hedging? Trying to wriggle out of the bargain? Meanwhile taking what amusement he could get on the side?

Her lip curled. Well, he wasn't going to use *her* again. She was wiser now. Not so vulnerable.

Or was she?

Though she took care not to look up, she was aware that his eyes seldom left her face. That steady regard was nerve-racking; it made her feel like some specimen on the end of a cruel pin.

The main course over, he removed the plates and helped her to a generous portion of apple pie and a piece of white Stilton.

So he'd remembered that she preferred cheese to cream with her apple pie, she thought as she glanced up unwarily, and met those brilliant, heavily lashed eyes. Twin candle flames were reflected in the black pupils, and, fascinated, mesmerised, she found herself unable to look away.

After what seemed an age, he broke the spell by saying conversationally, 'So tell me what's been happening since I last saw you.'

'I thought you were being kept informed,' she responded tartly.

Unruffled, he said, 'There are some important things I still don't know for sure. For example, why you ran away to Boston in the first place...'

Well, if he didn't know, she had no intention of telling him.

'I presumed it was because of Noel, that the pair of you had split when he discovered how you'd been two-timing him...'

He was a fine one to talk about two-timing, she thought bitterly.

When she said nothing, Rafe pursued, 'You certainly fooled me with that pretend shyness, that butter-wouldn't-melt routine.

'Though I should have realised by the way you disappeared at regular intervals with no explanation that you weren't the sweet innocent you pretended to be, nevertheless it came as quite a shock to discover just what kind of woman you were…'

Yes, she could still visualise his expression. He wasn't used to having the tables turned on him.

'So how many other men have you managed to fascinate and delude since then?' Rafe's question brought her back to the present with a bump.

When she looked at him mutely, he said, 'I know of at least one who wanted to marry you. Alan, I believe his name was.'

It must have been Eve who had told him, she realised. When she had mentioned Alan in her emails to Katie, it had been simply as a colleague.

'Did he get angry when he realised you'd been stringing him along? Is that why you came home?' His voice was full of resentment.

'I'm not in the habit of stringing men along,' she said stiffly.

'If you weren't stringing him along, why didn't you marry him?' he asked.

Madeleine's eyes dropped from his gaze. 'I didn't love him enough.'

'Not counting your husband, have you ever truly loved any man?'

A bitter, cold, gritty feeling in the centre of her chest brought such pain that Madeleine felt tears sting her eyes, and was forced to bend her head while she blinked them away.

He laughed mirthlessly. 'No, I thought not.'

'Well, you're wrong,' she flared, then, terrified he might have guessed, added with perfect truth, 'I've always loved Noel.'

'Clearly not enough, or you wouldn't have been happy to cheat on him… No, I'm afraid I don't *seriously* believe you've ever cared a jot about any man. Though there must have been plenty of men who loved you. Different men, but they were all drawn into the same old game, danced to the same old tune.' He moved to stand closer to her. 'But now those games are over, and, for the foreseeable future at least, I'll be the one calling the tune.'

'I—I don't know what you mean,' she stammered.

His little smile was like a breath of cold air on the back of her neck. 'I mean that everything has gone according to plan and you're here with me. Now all I have to do is *keep* you with me.'

'I might be stuck here for tonight because of the snow— which incidentally I don't believe even *you* could have arranged—'

With a wry grin, he said, 'I have to admit that the snow was fortuitous.'

'But I shall certainly be leaving first thing in the morning.' She tried to sound confident.

'I shouldn't bet on it.'

Going to the window, he drew aside the heavy red velvet curtains. Through the diamond-leaded panes she could see that thick snow, whipped along by a fierce wind, was swirling past.

'The previous owner admitted that during a bad winter this area, and the hall, can be snowed up for days at a time,' he added.

While her skin crawled with apprehension, she made a determined effort to put the situation on a more prosaic footing. 'Wouldn't you find being snowed up very inconvenient?'

'Just at the moment I find it the exact opposite,' he answered smoothly.

She ignored that, and, taking a deep breath, ploughed on determinedly. 'What made you decide to move to the country?'

'I was tired of living in town. I'd always intended to move to a rural area when the right house came on the market…'

Madeleine was surprised; she had always thought of Rafe

as a sophisticated city man. But then she had been wrong about so many things.

'As soon as I saw this place I knew it was what I'd been waiting for.'

'So you gave up your flat at Denver Court?'

'No, I still have it. It comes in handy for the odd night or weekend I want to spend in town.'

Relaxing a little, and determined to lighten the mood, she asked, 'Don't you find commuting a pain?'

'Not really. These days I work from home a good deal of the time. When I need to go into London I use a small chopper I pilot myself.'

'I didn't know you had a pilot's licence.'

He swished the curtain to, then suddenly he was by her side, looming over her. 'There are a lot of things you don't know about me. A lot you still have to learn.' A brittleness to his voice, he went on, 'For instance, I don't like being made a fool of by any woman, especially one I imagined loved me…'

The tension suddenly tightening like a hempen noose around her throat, she gazed up at him with wide, greeny-blue eyes. 'That's why I inveigled you here.'

That answered the first of her questions, but not the second. 'I can't imagine what you hope to gain,' she burst out agitatedly.

'Can't you?'

Watching her bite her lip, he glanced in the direction of the thick sheepskin rug. 'Shall we move in front of the fire and—?'

Flinching away, she cried hoarsely, 'No!'

He raised a dark, mocking brow. 'Anyone would think I was about to strip you naked and have my wicked way with you.'

When, her heart pounding against her ribs, she said nothing, he added softly, 'But that comes later…'

'If you lay a finger on me, I'll scream.'

He clicked his tongue. 'How melodramatic. Unfortunately, there's no one to hear you.'

'There's Mrs Boyce and her husband.'

'They've retired for the night... And, as their accommodation is several hundred yards away, above the old stable block, you'd have to scream very loudly indeed.'

She swallowed, her throat tight and dry. 'There must be other servants...'

'What staff I have live in modern bungalows on the estate. I'm afraid we're quite alone, so screaming would be useless.

'In any case, it's unnecessary at the moment. I was only going to suggest that we had our coffee in front of the fire.'

Feeling a little foolish, and realising vexedly that that was what he'd intended, she crossed to the hearth and sat down on the big leather couch while he collected the glass coffee jug from the hotplate.

Surely this was just some cat-and-mouse game he was playing in order to frighten her? she thought distractedly. And if it was, all she needed to do was keep calm and refuse to be frightened.

Which was easier said than done.

And if it wasn't?

No, she couldn't let herself think that way. There was only tonight to get through.

Only?

Then tomorrow morning she would find *some* way of leaving, she promised herself, even if she had to abandon her cases and walk...

'Planning your escape?'

She jumped, and as her colour started to rise he laughed. 'I've hit the nail on the head if that blush is anything to go by.'

How could he walk in and out of her mind like that? she wondered agitatedly as she accepted the cup of coffee he handed her.

He sat down beside her and, as though answering her question, went on, 'You have a very expressive face. Just then you looked fiercely determined…

'But I remember when you used to look eager and expectant, full of anticipation, hungry with desire and passion. Then afterwards, soft and dreamy, sated with love…'

'Stop it!' she cried.

He raised an eyebrow. 'Does the remembrance make you uncomfortable? As you profess to have loved Noel, do you regret two-timing him?'

'I regret ever meeting you,' she cried.

'Life's full of regrets. When we were in bed together, did you ever think of him? Regret that he wasn't the one holding you, making love to you?'

'Many times,' she flashed and, seeing the way his mouth tightened, realised with a feeling of triumph that she'd scored a hit, even if it was only his pride that was hurt.

'Was Alan a good lover?'

Rattled by the unexpected question, she answered sharply, 'That's nothing to do with you.'

'How many other men have you had apart from him?'

'How many other women have you had apart from—?' About to say 'Fiona', she brought herself up short.

'Apart from…?' He raised an eyebrow at her.

When she said nothing, he suggested, 'You? Well, I—'

She shook her head violently. 'I don't want to know. I really don't care.'

In truth, the idea of him making love to another woman still had the power to hurt. But his question had smacked far too much of the pot calling the kettle black.

Slowly, he said, 'I can't say I've lived like a monk, Madeleine, but neither am I any Casanova. One woman in my life is enough…'

You could have fooled me, she thought bleakly.

'But not just any woman will do. In fact my bed's been empty for quite a while…'

If that was the truth, where was Fiona? Unless she was once again in some clinic?

'The only thing I've had to warm it has been the dream of having you there…'

Though she knew now how faithless he was, her heart seemed to turn over in her breast.

Unable to stand any more, she put her coffee-cup down so that it rattled in the saucer and jumped to her feet. 'I'm going up to the flat.'

'Not just yet.' He caught her wrist and, before she could brace herself, pulled her onto his lap and held her there, both hands encircling her waist.

After a moment's useless struggle she sat stiff and straight, her head turned away.

'Relax,' he said, looking at the pure curve of her cheek. 'At one time you used to enjoy sitting on my lap in front of the fire… Especially if I—'

'Well, now I'd hate it!' she flashed.

'If I weren't a perfect gentleman I might move my hands a few inches higher and see whether or not that's the truth.'

Alarm made her heart race with suffocating speed. Her voice hoarse, she said, 'You'd be wasting your time. As far as you're concerned, I'm immune.'

'I'm not sure I believe you. Your heart's already beating faster, which, as you swore you weren't afraid of me, suggests that you want me.'

'I don't want you. I don't love you.'

'You didn't love me then, but you're a very passionate woman and your body always responded to mine without reservations.'

As she made to shake her head, he said, 'Don't bother to deny it. There are certain signs that couldn't be faked. It's something I'm sure of, and I don't believe that's altered. I could easily make you want me…give you a lot of pleasure…'

Boldly, she rejoined, 'My body *possibly*…but not my mind…and you once told me that a lot of sexual pleasure is generated in the mind…

'Now I'd like to go to bed.'

'Exactly where I want you.' Taking the pins from her hair, so that it tumbled round her shoulders in a pale cloud, he added softly, 'It's high time you made some reparation.'

Jolted, she asked through stiff lips, 'What is there to make reparation for?'

'No man likes to be made a fool of, to be taken for a ride then shrugged off—'

'I didn't—' she began.

'Oh, come! When your long-term lover returned to England you couldn't get rid of me fast enough. I have to say it rankled… Now I expect you to make up for it…'

So he was out for revenge, out to satisfy his wounded pride.

Her voice choked, she said, 'I don't want to go to bed with you. I *won't* go to bed with you.' Then in desperation, 'You can't force me to do anything I don't want to do.'

'I've no intention of using force. It won't be necessary.' He sounded so sure of himself.

Shudders running through her, she begged, 'Oh, please, Rafe, don't do this to me. I want to sleep in my own bed…alone…'

When he released her, hardly daring to believe she'd won, Madeleine struggled to her feet.

Rising at the same time, he put a light hand at her waist. 'I'll see you up.'

Very conscious of his hand in the small of her back, she was partway across the hall when he stopped her, and said quizzically, 'I'm afraid I can't bring myself to kiss Mary, and it's a shame to waste it.'

As he turned her into his arms and tilted her chin, she caught sight of the mistletoe hanging over them. A second later everything was wiped from her mind as his mouth covered hers.

Though his kiss was light to begin with, it had a devastating effect on her, and, shaken to the very core, she parted her lips beneath his the way a flower opened to the sun.

He made a sound almost like a groan and, running his fingers into her hair, deepened the kiss, taking his own sweet time, until her head was spinning.

There was nothing in the world but this man, his lips, his arms, the warmth and strength of his body, the memories of how it had been, and what he'd once meant to her.

When he finally freed her mouth, blind and dizzy, she swayed and clung to him.

He steadied her, then, lifting her high in his arms, carried her up the stairs. It was like something that was happening in a dream, something she was experiencing, yet not quite real.

When he set her down and flicked on the light she saw that she was in a strange room, a masculine room with a dark blue and white decor, a central chandelier and a king-sized four-poster bed with a blue and silver canopy.

'You told me you wanted to sleep alone in your own bed. If you still want that, you're free to go.'

Her whole body crying out for him, she could feel the heat running through her, the passionate hunger, the overwhelming need.

She knew with blinding clarity that she was still in love with him, and no matter that he didn't love her, no matter that he just wanted to use her, he was the only man she would ever love. She was forever tied to him.

'Do you still want that?' he repeated.

No!

She wasn't sure whether she'd spoken the word aloud, or

whether he'd read her surrender, but, his eyes never leaving her face, he began to strip off his clothes.

Her throat dry, her heart beating fast, she stood wide-eyed and defenceless, as if bewitched, and watched him.

He discarded his shoes and socks before taking off and tossing aside the black sweater. Then slowly he unfastened the belt of his trousers, dealt with the clip and zip, slid them down over lean hips and stepped out of them. A moment later his dark silk boxer shorts followed.

Naked, he sat on the edge of the bed and said, as he'd once said before, but this time it was a command, 'Take off your clothes for me.'

With trembling fingers, she began to strip off her things—shoes, stockings, dress and slip. When she reached behind her to unfasten her bra he got to his feet and, gripping her hands, trapped them there. Then he smiled into her eyes, and bent his head to put his mouth to her breast.

Through the delicate lace of the low-cut cups she could feel the heat and dampness, and her nipples firmed, needing more, aching for the exquisite sensations his mouth and tongue could bestow.

She tried to free her hands, but he wouldn't allow it. Instead he traced the upper curve of her breast with his tongue, coming tantalisingly close, but carrying on to the valley between and the other breast without giving her what she craved.

Then, holding both her wrists with one hand, he used the thumb of his free hand to stimulate without satisfying, while his mouth worked its way up to the warm hollow at the base of her throat and lingered there sensually.

Then suddenly she was free and he was back on the bed, watching her with green eyes that had gone dark and smoky.

She tossed aside the bra and slid the matching panties down over slender hips.

'Come here,' he ordered softly.

When she went to him he turned her round and pulled her down between his spread knees. Then, sliding his hands beneath her arms, he began to fondle her small, well-shaped breasts.

She could feel the roughness of his legs against her thighs and his firm flesh pressing urgently against the base of her spine. Even so, he seemed to be in no hurry, but to enjoy pleasuring her.

In the cheval-glass opposite she could see the pair of them reflected, the blonde head and the almost black, his tanned, muscular body in sharp male contrast to her pale, very womanly curves.

See what he was doing to her. How, his lean fingers dark against the creamy skin of her breasts, he was alternately stroking and teasing the dusky-pink nipples, pinching and tugging slightly, rolling each of them between a thumb and forefinger.

In some indefinable way the erotic sight added to the sensations, making them more intense.

Just when she thought she couldn't stand it a moment longer he slid one hand between her thighs, and with long, probing fingers drew all the exquisite sensations into a glorious whole.

When she jerked and began to shudder helplessly he put an arm around her and, drawing her back, held her more firmly against him. It was like holding a lit sparkler, all fire and light.

She was still quivering, still breathing fast when, his hands at her waist, he lifted her to her feet. 'Now let's see what you've learnt.'

Startled, she turned to look at him.

His green eyes mocking, he said, 'The days when women were expected to lie down and think of England are well and truly over. In these modern times women are men's sexual equals, so now it's your turn to make love to me.'

Stretching out indolently on his back, his hands clasped behind his head, he waited.

While her heart hammered against her breastbone, she dragged air into her lungs and, her hands unsteady, pushed back the long strands of blonde hair that were clinging damply to her cheeks.

'In the past you've always made a pretence of being a little shy and innocent,' he added caustically. 'Now you don't have to pretend any longer, so let's see what you know or what you've learnt since then.'

Her eyes filled with unspoken anguish and she bent her head and looked down, the overhead light casting the shadow of her long lashes onto her cheeks.

That look punched a hole in his heart.

He reached out and, taking her hand, squeezed it gently. A consoling gesture she remembered from the past. A gesture that now seemed to be merely mocking.

Snatching her hand away, she said raggedly, 'Very well, if that's what you want.'

When she awoke it was almost ten-thirty, and she was alone in the bed. While her body felt sleek and satisfied, her mind was a jumble of thoughts and mixed feelings.

After her somewhat clumsy attempt to make love to him, mortified by her own inexperience, she had been turning away when he stopped her.

'Let me go.' She tried to break free. 'I'm going back to the flat to spend the night.'

'I don't think so. It's too late.'

Suddenly he rolled and, reversing their positions, trapped her body beneath his. His weight sparked off a heated rush of desire that made her quiver.

Feeling that betraying movement, he put his mouth to her breast and felt her hips jerk in response.

As he recognised that her need was almost as great as his own, his lovemaking was hard and fast and intense, focused simply on the twin goals of pleasure and release.

Caught up in the dark glory of it, her breath ragged, she let go of the hurt and anger and abandoned herself.

This was real. This was enough.

Only it wasn't.

Despite the explosion of ecstasy, despite the bodily bliss, there was so much missing—the caring, the warmth, the commitment.

She started to cry, and the tears simply wouldn't stop.

He gathered her up and cradled her to him.

When she was all cried out, he kissed her wet cheeks and, holding her in the crook of his arm, settled her head on his shoulder.

Totally drained, emotionally exhausted, she slept almost at once.

In the early hours of the morning, still tangled in the gossamer threads of a lovely dream of a summer picnic she and Rafe had once shared, she reached out and touched him.

He stirred and turned his head, so that his face pressed into the curve of her neck.

Warm and sleepy, she snuggled against him and felt his immediate response, the hard hammer-blows of his heart as his arms closed round her. Then in the darkness his lips had found hers, and he was kissing her with a passion that once more set her alight.

They had kissed and caressed and made love a second time with an undiminished hunger, before falling asleep again in each other's arms.

Recalling the piercing beauty of their lovemaking, she felt her eyes fill with tears. She wept then for a lot of things. For past mistakes that couldn't be altered, for still loving him in spite of everything, but most of all for giving in and going to bed with him.

If she had been strong enough to hold out against him he wouldn't have forced her, she was sure of that. It was her own need for him that had been her downfall, that had wiped out this last year as if it had never been and left her once more in his thrall.

Despairingly she asked herself, how was it possible to go on loving a man who, once he'd had his revenge, for that was what it amounted to, wouldn't give her a second thought?

Even so, and though she despised herself, she knew that she might be tempted to stay and give him what he wanted from her, if only Fiona didn't exist…

But the other woman *did* exist and presumably *she* still loved Rafe in spite of everything. Still hoped to marry him.

Poor Fiona.

How was it possible for two women to go on loving a man who was basically rotten?

Three women, if she counted Harriet Rampling.

Out of the blue and for the first time, Madeleine found herself wondering about the relationship between Rafe and his godmother.

How was it that, after he had treated her daughter so shabbily, and apparently reneged on the bargain he had made with her husband, Harriet Rampling and her godson were still so close that she would choose to live in his house?

It didn't seem to make any sense.

CHAPTER SEVEN

MADELINE was drying her cheeks with the back of her hand when the bedroom door opened and Rafe came in carrying a tray of coffee.

He was wearing stone-coloured trousers and a fine olive-green sweater with a loose, sleeveless jerkin. His thick dark hair, a shade longer than was fashionable and trying to curl, was brushed back from a high forehead.

Needing to be in control, she sat upright and, pulling the duvet up to cover her nakedness, trapped it under her arms.

His eyes on her tear-stained face, he put the tray on the cabinet and, sitting down on the edge of the bed, reached out a hand to tilt her chin. 'Regrets?'

'It's too late for regrets.' In spite of all her efforts her voice shook betrayingly.

He freed a strand of hair caught in her earring, curled it round his finger and tucked it behind her ear, before cupping her cheek.

There was tenderness in his eyes, in his touch, and, feeling an uncontrollable wave of love, she turned her face into his palm.

The breath hissed through his teeth and then he was holding her close, his mouth muffled in her hair. 'I think it's about time we were—'

The trill of a phone cut through his words.

He drew back and, taking the mobile from his jerkin pocket, walked across to the window, saying over his shoulder, 'Don't let your coffee get cold.'

There were two cups on the tray, and, as she turned to pick up the coffee-pot and fill them, she heard him say a business-like, 'Lombard.'

A second later his voice changed to a softer, more caring tone. 'Hello, sweetheart, how are you…?'

Fiona, Madeleine realised, and something inside her shrivelled up.

'That's good… Yes…yes, that's right. No, I'm afraid we're snowed up, you wouldn't get here by road today. Probably not tomorrow, either…'

Her heart starting to race, Madeleine wondered if perhaps the other woman was in some clinic, and wanting to come home for Christmas?

'Yes, that would be fine,' Rafe agreed. 'I'll make the arrangements. As a matter of fact it will fit in very nicely with my other plans…'

If Fiona *was* intent on coming here, somehow *she* had to get away. The panicky thought was going through her mind when he added, 'I'll ring you back in a little while… Yes, yes, I will… Bye.'

He dropped the phone back into his pocket and returned to sit on the bed, making the mattress depress beneath his weight.

She was taken completely by surprise when he asked casually, 'How do you feel about a trip to London?'

'A trip to London?' she echoed blankly.

'I thought we might have lunch at the Denaught.'

'Lunch at the Denaught… But I—I thought…' She stammered to a halt.

'That I meant to keep you a virtual prisoner?'

Annoyed by his amusement, she demanded, 'Wasn't that what you intended me to think?'

Taking a sip of his coffee, which he liked black and sugarless, he admitted blandly, 'I did mention keeping you with me. But I was hoping to rely on persuasion rather than actual physical confinement.'

Wondering what kind of game he was playing, why he'd suggested having lunch out, she said, 'Didn't you just say we were snowed up?'

'To all intents and purposes we are. But we have a small snowblower that Jack can use to keep the helicopter pad clear. Ever been in a chopper?'

'No.'

'Fancy the idea?'

The true answer was no. She was afraid of heights and didn't much care for flying in any form. But it would be a chance to leave the house. A chance, once they were at the Denaught, to escape. If she excused herself to go to the powder room, hopefully she could get a taxi and be away before he missed her.

Trying to keep the excitement out of her voice, she readjusted the duvet and said, 'Yes, that would be very nice.'

'Of course, I'll want your word that you won't try to run. That you'll stick with the role of the physiotherapist Harriet hired.'

Try as she might she was unable to meet his eyes and, with a hark back to childhood, the hand hidden beneath the duvet had the first and middle fingers crossed as, after the briefest hesitation, she agreed, 'Very well.'

'Good. Then while you shower and dress I'll have a word with Jack and get everything organised.'

The second the door had closed behind him, she jumped out of bed, pulled on her clothes and hurried along the corridor to her flat.

As soon as she had dried herself and dressed she put on her make-up and coiled her hair, leaving the same small gold hoops in her ears that she'd worn the previous night.

She couldn't wait to get away. It would mean leaving her cases, but once she was safely in London she could arrange to have them picked up. In the meantime, Eve would lend her whatever she needed.

Dressed in a cream blouse and a fine wool suit the colour of molasses, she pulled on a pair of matching suede boots and crept downstairs.

As soon as she'd found Mrs Boyce and retrieved her handbag, she would go back to the flat and phone Eve.

There was no sign of the housekeeper, and, having peered into several rooms, including the kitchen, she was returning to the hall when Rafe appeared wearing a hip-length leather jacket.

'Lost?' he queried.

'I was looking for Mrs Boyce.' Instinctively she spoke the truth.

'Mary's off until after Christmas. Annie will be filling in for her, when she gets here.'

'Oh…' Madeleine said. But, thinking back, she could vaguely remember Mrs Boyce mentioning it.

'Were you wanting the housekeeper for any particular reason?' he asked.

Doing her best to sound casual, she explained, 'Last night I couldn't find my handbag. I thought I must have left it in the living room, but when I went to look it wasn't there. I presume Mrs Boyce must have found it and put it somewhere safe.'

'Well, if that's all it is, there's no problem.'

'But I need my purse and—'

He smiled lazily. 'Don't worry, I promise I'll buy lunch. Now, about ready to start?'

There was money in her flight bag, and she would need money for a taxi. Her mind working overtime, she said, 'Not quite… I'd better fetch a coat,' and fled back upstairs.

It was a moment's work to unpack her cream coat, and her

flight bag was where she'd left it. Knowing how useful its contents would be, she hesitated, sorely tempted to take it.

But the last thing she wanted to do was alert Rafe. Giving up the idea, she unzipped it and felt for the money she'd slipped into the inner pocket alongside her passport and other papers.

The pocket was empty.

It must be the one on the other side.

That too was empty.

Feeling as though she'd been kicked in the solar plexus, she made a more thorough search.

Everything else was there, but her money, her passport and other travel documents were gone.

Suddenly it all added up.

There were money and papers missing, a phone that wasn't working, no keys in the doors, a handbag that had mysteriously disappeared...

Realising that the whole thing had been carefully planned, she clenched her teeth.

'Got a problem?'

Looking up, she found Rafe was standing in the doorway, watching her.

Her voice tight with barely controlled anger, she began with the least important. 'The phone up here isn't working...'

'So Mary said,' he agreed blandly.

'There are no keys to the doors, and, before you try to fob me off with excuses, I know they've been purposely removed...'

Those lazy green eyes regarded her calmly. 'Then presumably you know why?'

'Oh, yes, I know why. To prevent me locking myself in, and to enable you to come in and out whenever it suits you—which you've no right to do...!'

'It *is* my house,' he pointed out when she paused to draw breath.

'It might be your house, but that doesn't give you the right to walk in and take my belongings…' she said breathlessly.

When he simply stood there and watched her, her voice shaking, she accused, 'You came in while I was asleep—' recalling the dream that the slight noise he must have made had triggered off, she shuddered, before going on '—and you stole my handbag and the money and papers from my flight bag. Don't bother to deny it.'

'I wasn't going to deny it,' he said mildly. 'Though *stole* is hardly the correct word. I'm merely keeping them safe until I'm satisfied you don't intend to do anything silly.'

'How dare you?' she cried hoarsely. 'You've no right to treat me like this—'

'Perhaps we could leave the recriminations until later? The chopper's warming up ready and Jack will be standing around waiting for us.'

Then, with a glance at her mutinous face, 'Unless you've changed your mind about going? If you have, we could always stay at home.'

She had opened her mouth to say that she had no intention of going anywhere with him, when she hesitated. There would be no chance of escaping if they stayed here. Better to put on a reasonably amicable front and go with him. Then at the first opportunity she would slip away. Either Eve or Noel would pay her taxi fare…

'Well?'

'I haven't changed my mind.'

Picking up her coat, he helped her into it. 'Then let's go.'

Outside it was a perfect winter's day, with a cloudless sky as blue as lapis lazuli. Though the sun shone brightly, the air was glacial, and frost sparkled like glitter on a Christmas card.

Snow covered everything in a thick white counterpane, filling in hollows, redefining the landscape, piling on sills and ledges, burying shrubs and plants, clothing bare branches and weighing down the green arms of the pine.

The apron outside the front door had been partially cleared and, harnessed to what appeared to be a child's sleigh, a small, sturdy pony waited placidly.

'Courtesy of the previous owner, who was going to live in Australia,' Rafe explained as he helped Madeleine into the sleigh and fitted himself in beside her.

Pressed as they were, hip to hip and thigh to thigh, there was just enough room for the two of them.

'It belonged to his children... Cosy, wouldn't you say?'

Robbed of breath by such close contact, Madeleine said nothing.

'We do have a snowmobile,' he went on, 'but there's something wrong with the engine and Jack is having to work on it.'

Finding her voice, she asked, 'How far is it to the helicopter pad?'

'Only a few hundred yards. But considering the conditions, I thought this mode of transport might be preferable to walking, and Jack says Hercules can do with some exercise.'

He made a clicking noise with his tongue, and apparently eager to live up to his name, Hercules set off with a will.

Though the sleigh ran easily enough, the pony's short legs sank into the snow alarmingly until they got under the lee of a wall bordering the path to the flat, raised ground where the helicopter pad and hangar were situated.

Looking for all the world like a plastic bubble, the helicopter was waiting, its door open, its rotor blades turning gently.

Jack came to meet them and take charge of the sleigh while Rafe, a hand at her waist, escorted her across to the small silver machine.

After a momentary hesitation, she ducked her head and climbed in.

Rafe closed the door and, a moment later, swung in beside her. Then, having fastened both their seat belts, he put on the headset and turned his attention to the controls.

The engine note rose to a whine and a second or so later, the downdraught from the rotor blades whipping up the surrounding powdery snow, they lifted off into the blue, blue sky.

As they levelled out Rafe glanced sideways at her, noting her absolute stillness, the slim hands clasped into fists, the way her eyes were fixed blindly on the control panel.

'OK?' he asked above the engine noise.

She nodded without moving her gaze.

Reaching out, he took the nearest hand and squeezed it reassuringly.

She gave him a small, wavering smile.

'That's my girl.'

After a minute or so she took a deep breath and forced herself to look down. She was rewarded by a truly fantastic view. A winter wonderland of glistening snow, a montage of fields and hedgerows and silver filigree trees.

Fascinated, she began to pick out small dwellings and isolated farms, streams and roads, and clearly, on the smooth white snow, the tracks of animals.

Then in no time at all, it seemed, the countryside gave way to town and they were coming in to land on the Denaught's clearly marked helicopter pad.

With its high grey stone walls, its towers and turrets and battlements, the place looked more like a castle than a hotel, Madeleine thought.

On the same wavelength, as he so often was, Rafe raised his voice to tell her, 'Long before it became one of London's top hotels, the Denaught was a fortified country house belonging to Sir Ian Bolton.

'After the Bolton family died out, the place stood empty for a time until some property developer realised its potential.'

When they touched down and the rotor blades slowed, he removed his headset and, unfastening their seat belts, queried, 'So how do you feel about your first helicopter flight?'

She surprised herself by saying, 'I enjoyed it. I hadn't expected to, as I'm terrified of heights.'

'It's somewhat different from standing on the edge of a precipice.'

'I pictured it as being just as terrifying.' She laughed.

'But still you came.' His voice was dry.

She hoped he hadn't guessed what she had in mind. It would make getting away all the more difficult, if he had.

But if the worst came to the worst, she would refuse point blank to go back with him. And if he tried to force her she would kick up a fuss, she decided as he came round to help her out.

The Denaught appeared to be very busy, and she was greatly cheered to see a red-coated doorman dealing with a steady trickle of taxis arriving at, and leaving, the main entrance.

There was much less snow here, a mere carpet compared to the thick covering they'd left behind them, which made walking easy even in fashion boots.

'Better make the most of it,' Rafe said, when she remarked on the fact. 'If the forecast is right, we've more heavy snow coming overnight, with blizzards in our neck of the woods…'

'Good afternoon, Mr Lombard…madam…' A youngish, round-faced man in a smart navy-blue uniform appeared from nowhere. 'Lovely day.'

'It is indeed,' Rafe answered.

'If you and the lady want to go straight in, I'll take care of things.'

'Thanks, Steve.'

'You seem to be well-known here,' she remarked, as they made their way across the concreted area and through a side-entrance.

'Yes, it's a place I often use. Apart from the fact that they have an excellent chef, the helicopter pad is extremely useful, and I keep a car here,' he added nonchalantly.

As they reached the foyer, with its crackling log fire and seasonal decorations, a grey-haired, distinguished-looking man wearing a cream carnation in his buttonhole, bore down on them.

'Good afternoon, Mr Lombard…'

'Afternoon, Charles. This is Miss Knight.'

'Miss Knight…' Obviously one of the old school, the manager made her a courteous little bow.

'I must apologise for giving you so little notice, at a peak time,' Rafe said.

Charles waved away the apology. 'It's always a pleasure to have you here, Mr Lombard.'

As their coats were borne away by one of his minions, he added, 'Your usual table's ready, and your guest has arrived.'

Rafe nodded. 'Thanks.'

'The young lady's waiting for you in the private lounge.' He indicated a door to the right.

Madeleine's thoughts began to race as, a hand beneath her elbow, Rafe escorted her across the foyer towards the lounge.

Remembering his previous phone conversation, she felt hollow inside.

As Fiona couldn't get to the hall, had he suggested that they meet here?

But if he had, why had he included *her*? Unless he'd decided that she was safer under his eye than left to her own devices.

After all, he had no idea that she and Fiona had ever met, no idea that she knew about the bargain he had made with his godfather.

And she was hardly likely to tell the other woman how he'd tricked her into going to the hall. So perhaps he was hoping to present her simply in the role of physiotherapist?

The role he had asked her to play.

Another thought struck her. Did he mean to take Fiona back in the helicopter? Though how did he intend to extract 'reparation' from *her* with his fiancée on the scene…?

Well, whatever his intentions, if it was Fiona waiting in there, he had a nasty shock coming.

But if it was Fiona, she'd rather tell him the truth now than have to face the other woman.

At the door to the lounge, her insides churning, she dug her toes in and asked jerkily, 'Who is it that's waiting?'

'You'll see.'

'I'd like to know.'

Shaking his head, he said decidedly, 'That would spoil the surprise,' and, opening the door, propelled her inside.

She was aware of a log fire burning in what seemed to be a deserted room, before a small figure came hurtling towards her. Almost knocked off balance, she found herself being hugged with a warmth and enthusiasm that went straight to her heart.

'Katie!' she exclaimed, half laughing, half crying. 'How you've grown. You're getting really tall. You almost come up to my chin.'

'*You* haven't changed at all,' Katie declared. 'You're just as beautiful as ever.' She turned to Rafe and gave him a hug. 'Thank you for bringing her, Uncle Rafe.'

Then, taking Madeleine's hand, she went on happily, 'I'm so glad you're back. I've missed you. Aren't you pleased to be home?'

Glancing up, Madeleine met Rafe's ironic gaze. Dragging her eyes away, she said, 'Of course I am.'

'School's broken up for Christmas, so when Mum told me you were staying at the hall so you could treat Uncle George, I asked if I could come and see you. But Uncle Rafe said you were all snowed up…'

So it had been Katie Rafe had been talking to when he used the endearment *sweetheart*, not Fiona.

'Did you enjoy flying in the helicopter?' Katie asked eagerly.

'Yes, I quite liked it.'

'I thought you would,' the child said proudly. 'That's why I asked Uncle Rafe if he could bring you to see me.'

So though he must have known he was running a risk, known that she might refuse to go back with him, he'd brought her to please Katie.

'He didn't tell me,' Madeleine said.

'I asked him not to say anything because I wanted to surprise you.'

'Well, you certainly did that.' She squeezed the child's hand. Then, puzzled, asked, 'But surely you didn't come alone?'

'No, Helga, the au pair, brought me. She'll be coming back for me at two o'clock…'

Which meant she would have to delay her escape, Madeleine realised. There was no way she could disappear while Katie was still here.

'Mum is at work,' the child went on. 'She's going to join us as soon as she can get away. But she said to start eating without her, just in case she can't make it for lunch.

'I'm hungry already. I was too excited to eat much break-fast. Are *you* hungry, Maddy?'

Still feeling churned up, Madeleine lied, 'Yes, I am.'

'Well, if my two favourite girls are hungry—' Rafe put an arm around each of them '—let's go and eat.'

Katie fairly danced along, her dark, glossy plait swinging. 'While we have lunch I can tell you all about Bertrand…'

When, seated by one of the long windows in the pleasant dining room, they had finished ordering, Madeleine asked, 'Who's Bertrand?'

'He's the Labrador that Uncle Rafe is giving me for Christmas. Though I'm fine again now, Mum and Dad don't want me to ride any more until I'm grown up, so they agreed I could have a dog. Bertrand's about six months old and I'm getting him tomorrow, because the sanctuary doesn't open on Christmas Day.

'I decided to call him Bertrand because that's Uncle Rafe's middle name…'

'Is it really?' Madeleine laughed. 'I didn't know that.'

Rafe grimaced. 'Not a lot of people do.'

Then to Katie, 'Do you *have* to tell all my most shameful secrets? And come to that, how do you know?'

The little girl giggled. 'Mum told me. But she thinks Bertrand is rather grand for a puppy, so I'll probably call him Bertie for short.' She turned her attention back to Madeleine. 'He was rescued when his previous owner left him shut in the basement of a derelict house,' she explained. 'He'd almost starved to death before he was found. But he's very friendly and he still likes people.

'He's from the Mill House Animal Sanctuary. Uncle Rafe gives them lots of money to help the animals…'

While they waited for the meal to be served, and between courses, Katie chatted away non-stop.

Madeleine smiled and listened and marvelled that a child she had regarded as quiet and a little shy could be so talkative.

Catching her eye, Rafe said with a wry smile, 'As a rule Katie doesn't say much, but when she gets excited she could talk for England.'

They had almost finished their coffee before Diane herself came hurrying in, wearing a businesslike grey suit and carrying a black shoulder-bag-cum-briefcase. Her cheeks were flushed and she sounded more than a shade breathless as she said, 'Hi there.'

'You're very late, Mum,' Katie pointed out.

'Yes, I know, darling, and I'm sorry. I began to think I wasn't going to make it at all. I was trapped into having lunch with a client.'

She gave her brother, who had risen at her approach, a peck

on the cheek and, stooping to hug Madeleine, said with obvious sincerity, 'It's good to have you back.'

'I expect you can do with some coffee?' Rafe asked.

'You're a mind-reader.' Dropping into the chair he'd pulled out for her, Diane smoothed a hand over the dark hair that fell straight and gleaming to her shoulders, and grumbled, 'Sometimes I wonder why I keep on working.'

He smiled. 'You know perfectly well that you love your work. If you didn't have it, you'd be lost.'

'That's true. I just don't want to be a mirror image of Mother.'

He raised an eyebrow. 'I don't think you need to worry on that score.'

'But you wouldn't want *your* wife to have a career,' Diane noted.

'I'd prefer her not to. Unless it would make her seriously unhappy to give it up. If that was the case, I'd have to withdraw my opposition...' He sat back confidently.

They chatted for a minute or so until the fresh coffee had arrived and been poured, before Katie reminded him, 'Uncle Rafe, you promised you'd show me the inside of your helicopter some time and let me sit in the pilot's seat...'

'Well, I will, sweetheart.'

'Can't you do it now?' She glanced at her watch. 'It's only a quarter to two.'

As Rafe hesitated, Diane said, 'Go if you want to. Maddy and I can catch up on some gossip.'

'Oh, *please*, Uncle Rafe.' Katie was already on her feet and tugging at his arm.

He cast his eyes heavenwards. 'I should have more sense than promise these things.'

'Go on,' Diane urged, 'you know you want to.' Then to Madeleine, 'Men always enjoy showing off their toys.'

'Femaled into it,' he said with mock-resignation. 'Come on, then, Poppet. We'll pick up your coat on the way out.'

'It's Helga's yoga class this afternoon,' Diane reminded her daughter, 'so if you see her come while you're out there, you'd better go straight home with her. Daddy should be there by the time you get back.'

'All right… Bye, then, Mum.'

'Bye, darling. I won't be late tonight.'

'That's good. Bye, Maddy. Come and see us soon—then you'll be able to meet Bertie. I think you'll like him.' Katie ran back and put her arms round Maddy.

'I'm sure I will,' Madeleine agreed, and hugged the slight figure.

'Come on, then, Uncle Rafe…' She took his hand.

Over the child's head his eyes met Madeleine's, an unmistakable warning in their cool green depths, as he said lightly, 'I'll be back in ten minutes or so. Don't go anywhere.'

As the tall, broad-shouldered man and the slender dark-haired child turned away, they heard Katie coax, 'If I'm very careful, will you let me try on the earphones, Uncle Rafe?'

He smiled down at her. 'I dare say.'

'Oh, goodie!'

While the pair made their way to the door, Diane sipped her coffee and looked after them fondly. 'I'll be pleased when Rafe settles down and has a family of his own…'

Madeleine felt her heart constrict as if an iron band had tightened round it as Diane added, 'He'll make a really good father. He's great with Katie, and she fairly dotes on him.' Then a shade diffidently, 'I hadn't realised how things were—between you and Rafe, I mean—until he told me…'

Madeleine found herself wondering exactly how much he'd told his sister, and where Fiona fitted into all this. It didn't sound as if Diane knew about the bargain Rafe had struck with his godfather… Or if she did, she certainly didn't seem to be blaming him for not keeping it.

'He hasn't been happy while you've been away,' Diane

went on. 'But now you're back, thank the lord, and I'm only too delighted that things finally look like they're working out…'

Not knowing what to say, Madeleine stayed silent.

'Poor Rafe… In some ways he's had a raw deal…'

Seeing the sceptical look on Madeleine's face, she hurried to defend her brother. 'Oh, yes, I know he *appears* to be the man who has everything, but so far, through no fault of his own, he's lost out in ways that have really mattered to him.

'Though he was never deprived of material possessions, he didn't have a very happy childhood. In fact it's a miracle he didn't grow up warped…'

Recalling the story he'd told her about his stepfather, Madeleine began, 'You mean…?'

'I mean he could so easily have ended up weak, psychologically damaged. But thank the lord he's turned out to be one of the strongest, most stable people I know.

'The only thing I've ever known to really throw him off balance was when you went to the States…' She glanced up at Madeleine and then went on, 'But to get back to the point. Our mother wasn't a home-maker. She never wanted children. She was a career woman through and through, and well over thirty when she married Dad. Even then she only agreed to a wedding because I was on the way.

'Children bored her, and she couldn't wait to get me off her hands so she could be free. Unfortunately for her, there was still Rafe to come.

'She believed she was in the menopause, and by the time she found she was pregnant again, it was too late to do anything about it. No child asks to be born, yet, as though he was to blame, she always resented him.

'Dad and I did our best, but he needed a mother's love, and the more he tried to get close to her, the more she pushed him away. He was much too young to understand why…'

Madeleine's heart bled for the poor, bewildered child who'd been so cruelly rejected. But after the way he'd treated Fiona he didn't deserve her pity, she reminded herself.

'Then when he was twelve and I was nineteen our father died, and six months later, to our surprise, Mother remarried. Unlike Dad, who was a kind man and wouldn't have hurt a fly, her new husband was a brute and a bully. It's not surprising that Rafe came to hate him…

'To cut a long story short, when Rafe was barely fourteen, for his own safety, he was sent to live with his godparents.'

Her face clouded.

'It's true that they welcomed him with open arms, but even there he had his share of problems…'

Madeleine was taken aback. When Rafe had talked about his godparents, he'd made no mention of any problems. Rather he'd emphasised how well they'd treated him.

As if pushing aside unpleasant memories, Diane made a dismissive gesture and went on, 'Though at that time the Charns could well afford it, he was anxious not to be a financial burden. He wanted to be independent, to be able to fund his own schooling.

'As though in answer to a prayer, when our paternal aunt died she left us a small legacy in her will. I used my half to further my career, while Rafe, with his godfather's help and approval, put his into stocks and shares.

'When it comes to finance, my brother has the Midas touch. Everything he invested in turned to gold, and by the time he went to university he had the independence he craved.

'He could have cut free then from the Charn household, but he didn't,' Diane said proudly. 'He continued to call their house home, continued to treat them as if they were his own parents. And when Christopher ran into trouble, Rafe stood by him through thick and thin…'

Well, he would do if he was expecting to inherit Charn Industries, Madeleine thought cynically. But once again there had been no mention of Fiona.

She was about to jump in with both feet and ask where the other woman was, when Diane exclaimed, 'Oh, lord, aren't I rabbiting on? But I wanted you to know, to understand, that Rafe isn't—'

'Isn't what?' Rafe asked.

Both women jumped.

'Oh, you're back,' Diane said. And, obviously flustered to be caught talking about him, hurried on, 'Did Katie enjoy the helicopter?'

He grinned. 'Enormously. She's quite determined to get a pilot's licence as soon as she's old enough.'

'I take it she's gone?'

'Yes. Helga was running a few minutes late, otherwise she would have stopped for a word.'

Diane picked up her shoulder-bag. 'Speaking of being late, I'll have to get a move-on myself. Thanks for the coffee.' She turned back to her brother. 'We'll be at home all over Christmas. Stuart's mum and dad are coming to stay with us, so you must bring Madeleine for a meal as soon as you can make it.'

'Will do.'

'Keep in touch, and let me know how things are.' Glancing at her watch, she added, 'I've got an appointment at three-fifteen, so I'll have to dash. But first I must pop into the ladies' room and check my make-up.'

'I'll come with you.' Madeleine seized her chance as Diane gave Rafe a sisterly kiss.

Then, leaving him to signal a waiter and pay the bill, the two women walked back to the main lobby. Though her heart was thudding, Madeleine tried hard to appear casual, in case he was watching them.

As soon as Diane was safely out of the way, she'd slip outside and ask the doorman to get her a taxi. It would mean leaving without her coat, but that was a small price to pay, and no doubt Eve would be able to lend her one.

CHAPTER EIGHT

THE blue and gold powder room was momentarily deserted. Meeting Diane's green eyes in the mirror and watching her run a comb through her hair, Madeleine took a deep breath and broached the subject that had been weighing so heavily on her mind.

'I was wondering about Fiona...'

As the other woman began to apply a fresh coat of lip gloss, Madeleine hurried on, 'Is she all right now? I understand that she had a lot of problems in the past...'

'Lord, did she have problems! The whole family were worried sick about her, but because she'd always clung to Rafe he bore the brunt of it. Now she's doing fine, I'm pleased to say. When she was finally given a clean bill of health it must have taken a great weight off his mind as well as Harriet's. I know it did off mine... Well, I really must fly or I'm going to be dreadfully late. Take care. See you soon...' Diane waved goodbye.

Madeleine sighed. After all that, she was little wiser. The only thing she knew for certain was that Fiona was well, and not languishing in some clinic.

The most important questions remained unanswered. Was she still hoping to marry Rafe? Still hoping that he would keep his part of the bargain? But if that was the case, why wasn't she with him?

As Diane hurried out, a small group of women came in, laughing and talking.

It occurred to Madeleine that if she waited until they went out and mingled with them she would be a lot less conspicuous if Rafe was keeping an eye on the lobby.

They seemed to take an age, and she made a pretence of re-coiling her hair and checking her make-up while she waited on tenterhooks.

When the group finally headed for the door she joined their ranks and slipped out with them.

She had half feared Rafe would be waiting, but a hasty glance around the lobby showed no sign of him.

With a sigh of relief she hurried to the main entrance, where a door with panels of thick stained glass was opened for her by the red-coated doorman.

There were vehicles coming and going, and a silver Mercedes was drawn up a few paces away, its engine idling. But there seemed to be no cabs.

'Can you call me a taxi, please?' she asked, aware that she sounded breathless.

'Certainly, madam.'

As he moved to do her bidding, Rafe appeared by her side, her coat over his arm. 'That won't be necessary, James. The lady's with me.'

'Right, Mr Lombard.'

While shock kept her rigid, motionless, he slipped a note into the doorman's hand and put her coat around her shoulders.

She had drawn breath to tell him she had no intention of going back with him, when he tipped her face up and, letting his thumb graze along her jawline, said softly, 'I'm very well-aware that you had your fingers crossed.'

Though his voice was cool, careless, it held a bite that made her feel small. As the heat rose in her cheeks he smiled into her eyes and, bending his head, kissed her.

That sorcerer's mouth worked its black magic, scattering her wits and making her head reel. As if under a spell she allowed herself to be steered to the nearby car and installed in the front passenger seat.

He slid in beside her, clicked their seat belts into place, and they were away before she could catch her breath.

It was a good thirty seconds before she was able to think straight. Then she began to berate herself. Why had she weakly let him take charge of her again? Why had her fighting spirit, her determination to resist at all costs, died so easily? Why had she allowed her common sense to be submerged, her basic instinct of self-preservation to be swamped by the magic of his kiss?

Because she couldn't help it. She was held in thrall by her love for him.

It wasn't a comfortable thought. It stripped her of her freedom, her independence, even her pride, and put her at the mercy of a man who had treated his sick fiancée without any consideration.

Well, she wouldn't be put in that position. Somehow, she resolved, she would find the strength to fight, the strength to leave him…

They were pulling out of the hotel forecourt to join the main traffic stream before it occurred to her to wonder about their mode of transport.

Earlier, Rafe had talked as if the roads around Hethersage would be impassable for the next couple of days, so why were they going back by car rather than in the helicopter?

When she voiced the question, he answered calmly, 'We're not going back to Hethersage, at least not straight away. I'd like to go back tomorrow and have Christmas there, but right now I've plans which necessitate spending the night in town.'

'Spending the night in town?' She was surprised.

'Have you any objections?'

'No.' Being in London suited her just fine. It would give her a much better chance of carrying out her resolve than being snowbound at the hall.

But she couldn't help but wonder *why* he wanted to spend the night in town. Rafe wasn't a man to do anything without a good reason.

Perhaps it was something to do with Fiona. Thinking back to his phone conversation with Katie, she recalled him saying, 'As a matter of fact it will fit in very nicely with my other plans.'

Taking a deep, calming breath, she asked, 'What *are* your plans exactly?'

'As parking will be a nightmare, I intend to leave the car at Denver Court and take a taxi into the centre of town to do some shopping.'

'Shopping?' It was the last thing she had expected. He gave her a glinting sideways glance. 'For your birthday present, amongst other things…'

Her birthday… Even Eve and Noel hadn't remembered, and so much had happened in the past two days she hadn't given it a thought.

'How did you know it was my birthday?'

'You once mentioned that if you'd been born a few minutes *after* midnight instead of a few minutes *before*, your birthday would have fallen on Christmas Eve.'

And he'd remembered. Just for a moment she struggled against tears.

As though he sensed her emotion, he went on briskly, 'So what would you like for a present? It's up to you to choose.'

'I don't want a present from you.'

There was a telling silence, then she rushed into speech, 'I'm sorry if I sounded rude and ungrateful. I'm not ungrateful…'

'Just rude?'

Knowing she had been brought a flush to her face. Still she persevered, 'I really don't want you to buy me anything.'

As though she hadn't spoken, he said, 'It might be a good idea to start our shopping trip at Harrod's.

'As you haven't got either a handbag or an overnight bag with you, you'll need a number of things. A dress for this evening, accessories, underwear, night wear, toiletries, make-up…'

'But I—'

'Don't argue.'

'I don't want to be forced into having anything I can't pay for,' she informed him stiltedly. 'I hate to feel beholden.'

She saw by the way his beautiful mouth tightened that her words had angered him.

But as though striving to be reasonable, he said equably, 'Look on it as your Christmas present.'

'I don't want a Christmas present.' Flatly, she added, 'I can't afford to buy you one.'

'So indulge me, and call it your Christmas present to me.'

Little shivers started to run up and down her spine, as he added, 'Strictly speaking you won't *need* a nightdress… But we'll get one anyway, so I can have the pleasure of taking it off…'

London's busy streets and most of its pavements were clear of snow, but with frost laying icy fingers on everything, its parks and gardens and squares clad in bridal white, it looked an enchanted city as they headed towards Denver Court.

As well as apartments the complex had a small, select shopping mall, a comprehensive fitness centre, an indoor and an outdoor swimming pool, and two of the most exclusive and expensive restaurants in town, the Starlight Room and the Jacobean Room.

When they stopped at the main entrance to the court one of the security staff came over. 'Good afternoon, Mr Lombard. Nice to see you back.'

'Afternoon, John. Can you call a taxi, preferably one I can hire for the rest of the afternoon, and then take care of the car for me?'

'Consider it done.' A mobile phone appeared in his hand. After a brief conversation, he reported, 'Danny, who has his own cab, is just dropping a passenger. He'll be with you any minute.'

As Rafe helped Madeleine out and handed over the car keys a well-kept taxi appeared, and in a moment they were installed in it and heading for Knightsbridge and Harrod's.

Everywhere was crowded with last-minute shoppers, but miraculously both the human traffic and the vehicular managed to keep moving.

It was starting to get dusky, and in the centre of town the Christmas lights were just coming on.

Teddy bears wearing festive hats tumbled and clowned, Santas and sleighs, reindeer and elves, stars and angels blinked on and off, vying with glittering shop windows full of seasonal displays of wines and foodstuffs, furs and jewellery, toys and luxury goods.

On the street corner a Salvation Army band, the brass instruments gleaming under the lights, was playing carols, while one of its female members wielded a collecting box.

While their taxi was held up by a red traffic light, Rafe rolled down his window and passed her a wad of notes.

'Thanks,' she called. 'Happy Christmas.'

'You're very generous,' Madeleine remarked.

'I can afford to be, and I have great respect for the Salvation Army; they do a good job.'

When their taxi drew up outside Harrod's, whose window displays were a delight as always at this time of the year, having thanked the driver, Rafe asked, 'Can you find somewhere to park, then come back for us in…say…an hour?'

'Can do,' the man agreed laconically. 'But it'll cost a packet.'

'That's not a problem,' Rafe said smoothly, and more notes changed hands.

He turned to Madeleine and, shrugging out of his leather jacket, said, 'I suggest you leave your coat in the car; you won't need it.'

When, still unhappy about him spending money on her, she had reluctantly slipped out of her coat he hurried her into the huge store.

'We'll start in the dress department.'

Despite the crush of shoppers, focused and positive, Rafe got attention with no apparent effort.

Unlike most men he had very clear ideas about what would suit her and how he wanted her to look, and when, her mouth stubborn, she refused to choose, he chose for her.

In a remarkably short space of time she had everything he had previously listed, including an evening bag and a shoulder-bag. Amazingly, it was still a few minutes short of an hour when, loaded with boxes and packages, he shepherded her towards the main doors.

Just as they reached the pavement their taxi drew up, the lights gleaming on its polished bonnet.

When the packages were stored in the boot and she was settled in her seat, Rafe gave the driver an instruction she didn't catch and got in beside her.

As they pulled away from the kerb, he asked quizzically, 'There, that wasn't too painful, was it?'

Hating to be railroaded like that, she stayed mutinously silent.

He picked up her hand, which was clenched into a fist, and, straightening the fingers one by one, said, 'Tell me something; if you were my wife, or we were about to marry, would you still object to me buying you things?'

Her heart did a little flip before she answered, 'No, of course not. But that's different.'

Instead of just wanting to use her to satisfy his lust and

soothe his wounded pride, it would mean that he loved and respected her. It would change everything.

'As it is, I feel like a…a paid mistress.'

'That denigrates us both.' Though he spoke softly, she heard the edge of anger in his voice.

Responding to that anger, she said, 'I suppose you've never had to pay for sexual favours.'

'No, I haven't,' he replied curtly. 'And I wasn't thinking of starting now.'

Suddenly ashamed of herself, of her behaviour, she admitted, 'I shouldn't have said that. I'm sorry…'

With a little sigh, he lifted her hand to his lips and kissed the palm. 'And I'm sorry we didn't do the more important shopping first.

'Had we done things the other way round, it might have made all the difference to how you feel.'

She shook her head. 'I don't see how it could have made any difference.'

'Wouldn't that rather depend on what I was thinking of buying?'

Confused, she said, 'I don't know.' Then, curiously, 'What were you thinking of buying?'

'I'll tell you when we get there.'

Uneasy, she insisted, 'Tell me now.'

'Apart from your birthday present? A ring.'

'A r—ring?' she stammered.

'An engagement ring,' he said deliberately.

Once, when she had fondly imagined he might love her, that would have been like a dream come true. Now it was bewildering and unsettling.

'Why would you want to buy me a ring when you said all you wanted was reparation?'

'Shall we say for the look of the thing? So that other people—'

'I don't want a ring,' she broke in, her voice thick. 'It would just be a sham.'

'You've made it clear that you don't want to feel like a paid mistress. As my fiancée you would have no cause to feel that way, and while we're together you'd have a certain status.'

'You can keep your money. I don't need a ring. I've no intention of staying with you. Apart from the fact that you want revenge, I mean nothing to you—'

'I'm afraid you've become something of an obsession, and I've no intention of letting you go until I'm good and ready.'

'You can't *force* me to stay.'

'No,' he agreed, 'but you will. There's a part of you that *wants* to. A part of you that—at the risk of sounding melodramatic—is still in thrall. Otherwise you would never have slept with me last night, never have left the Denaught with me today.'

When, thrown by such an accurate assessment, she stayed silent, he went on, 'Maybe you need to get me out of your system, the same as I need to get you out of mine...'

Chilled by his words, she shivered.

'And the best way to do that, and set both of us free, would be to stay together until the torment, the fixation, the obsession, call it what you will, dies a natural death...'

If only it were that simple.

'Ah, here we are.' The taxi had drawn up outside Marshall Brand, one of the best known and most exclusive jewellers in town, whose windows invariably displayed the minimum of rare and beautiful objects.

'Can you give us half an hour or so?' Rafe asked the driver.

The man nodded. 'We're in luck. I've just spotted a free meter a few yards further on.'

Opening the door, Rafe jumped out, and before Madeleine could argue she found herself urged out of the taxi and across the pavement.

A uniformed security guard opened the heavy glass door and, after an assessing glance at Rafe, ushered them into the palatial shop.

With mirrored walls, crystal chandeliers and vases of fresh flowers, the sales area was set out like a salon. Velvet-covered couches and easy chairs, interspersed with elegant display cabinets and small glass-topped tables, were widely spaced on a thick, plum-coloured carpet.

As Madeleine glanced around her, a delicate gold bracelet in one of the cabinets caught her eye, and for a moment or two she was lost in admiration of its beauty and simplicity.

'Mr Lombard?' A well-dressed man with silver hair and rimless glasses appeared from nowhere.

Turning from watching Madeleine, Rafe said easily, 'That's right.'

'Good afternoon. I'm Carl Brand.'

The two men shook hands.

An arm at her waist, Rafe made the introduction. 'This is Miss Knight, my fiancée.'

'Miss Knight…' Carl Brand inclined his head.

'I'm sorry that we're somewhat later than I'd first anticipated,' Rafe said.

'Please don't apologise.' Brand waved them to the nearest couch. 'If you would care to take a seat, I have a selection of rings the size you indicated, ready to show you.'

As he proceeded to unlock the nearest display cabinet they heard a pop, and a young woman appeared with a still-smoking bottle of vintage champagne and two glasses on a silver tray.

When the flutes had been filled, feeling as though she was an actress in some play, Madeleine accepted one and took a sip. The wine was cool and sparkling, like quicksilver on her tongue.

While they sipped the champagne, half a dozen rings on

individual stands were placed on the table. There was a ruby, an emerald, a beautiful aquamarine on a chased gold band, a sapphire, a cluster of small, perfect opals and a huge diamond solitaire.

All were superb of their kind.

'I'll give you a moment,' Brand murmured, and moved discreetly into the background.

'What do you think, darling?' Rafe asked.

Caught on the raw by the *darling*, she wondered how he'd deal with it if she announced that she hated them all, and walked out.

But she very much doubted if she could drum up sufficient nerve.

As though he'd read her mind, he glanced at her, his green eyes holding an unmistakable warning, as he suggested, 'Suppose you try one on?'

'Do I have any other option?' she asked pleasantly.

He deliberately chose to misunderstand her. 'If you don't care for any of these, we can always ask to see some more.'

She shook her head. 'I don't want to see any more.'

'Does that mean there's one here you like?'

In the circumstances it didn't matter, though for her one particular ring stood out.

Unwilling to say so, she cooed with saccharine-sweetness, 'As you're buying it, *darling*, I'd much prefer you to choose.'

'Sure?'

'Sure.'

Though he smiled, she knew he was annoyed, both by her mockery and her refusal to co-operate.

'Very well.'

She felt a fleeting regret. He would probably insist on buying the diamond, her least favourite. Though she couldn't deny it was a magnificent ring, and many women would have preferred it, it was too large and showy for her taste.

Reaching out, he selected a ring and slipped it onto her finger. 'This would be my choice.'

Madeleine found herself staring down at the aquamarine as he added, 'It matches your beautiful eyes.'

It fitted to perfection, and looked wonderful on her slim, but strong, hand.

Had this been a real engagement it was the ring she would have chosen, and suddenly she found herself gazing at it through a mist of tears.

He tilted her chin, and she looked into his eyes, her own open wide, afraid to blink. Seeing the shimmer of tears, he said, 'Of course, if you have any other preference...'

She shook her head, mutely.

He kissed her lightly on the lips. 'In that case we'll take it.'

Soft-footed, Carl Brand returned to ask, 'Is there anything here that takes your fancy?'

'We've decided on the aquamarine.'

'An excellent choice, if I may say so. It's a particularly fine stone. The colour and clarity are superb, and it was cut by Jean Pierre Falgayras, a master craftsman. Would you like to have it wrapped?'

'I don't think so.' As Madeleine made to take it off, Rafe stopped her. 'Keep it on, darling. I'd like you to wear it.'

'At the moment it's still fully insured,' Brand told him. 'But if you want to check the details...'

'I don't think that's necessary.'

Rafe got to his feet and, taking the older man on one side, engaged him in a low-toned conversation.

'We can certainly do that, Mr Lombard,' Madeleine heard Brand agree. Then, 'We do indeed, and they come from the same house. If you'll give me a moment...'

He raised a hand and, when a young woman hastened over, issued a quiet instruction that had her hurrying away again.

She returned after a minute or so carrying a midnight-blue leather case, with Marshall Brand stamped in gold on the lid.

At a signal from Brand, she handed the case to Rafe and unobtrusively refilled the champagne glasses before moving away.

He opened it and, after scrutinising the contents, snapped it shut again, nodding his approval.

'Would you like that gift-wrapped?' Brand queried.

'Please.'

While Rafe and Carl Brand dealt with the financial side, Madeleine stared down at the aquamarine and sipped her champagne.

She felt strange and light-headed, a confusion of thoughts whirling through her brain like autumn leaves in a wind-storm.

Why had he insisted on her having a ring? Had he really been considering her status? How she would feel about being his unwilling mistress?

Oh, surely not. It just didn't add up. If all he wanted was reparation, why should he take *her* feelings into account?

Recalling what Diane had said about him being knocked off balance when she'd gone to Boston, she wondered if he might once have cared a little for her.

Obviously he no longer did, but he certainly *wanted* her. He'd admitted to being obsessed, admitted that he needed to be free of her…

Perhaps his idea was to try and get her out of his system before he married Fiona.

But if it was, it still didn't explain why he'd insisted on a ring.

And surely Fiona wouldn't be a party to another woman wearing his ring, even if it meant nothing…

Or would she?

If she wanted Rafe badly enough, and agreeing to do things on his terms was the only way she could get him, she might.

Madeleine sighed and, her mind shifting focus, began to consider things from another angle.

All this time she had blamed Rafe for treating Fiona so badly, for reneging on the bargain he had made. But perhaps if he hadn't met *her* when he did, if they hadn't become lovers, he would have gone ahead and married Fiona.

She wouldn't have deliberately taken another woman's man, but she had never asked if there was anyone else, merely presumed that there wasn't. So could part of the blame be laid at her door? It was a most unsettling thought. She had more than enough to feel guilty about.

Making a tremendous effort, she tried to clear away the confusion in her mind and decide what her course of action should be. Was she going to run at the first real opportunity? Or was she going to go down the bitter-sweet path of staying with Rafe whenever he wanted her?

No, she thought violently, with the shadow of Fiona still in the background, she couldn't do that.

But loving him as she did, could she find enough strength to walk away from him?

She still hadn't reached a decision when, carrying two gift-wrapped packages, Rafe returned to ask, 'All set to go?'

Wondering if one of them was for Fiona, she rose to her feet to accompany him.

They were escorted by Brand, who, at the door, wished her, 'A very happy birthday,' and put a small box wrapped in silver paper into her hand. She thanked him with a smile that made him her slave for life.

Outside a few flakes of snow were drifting down, adding a touch of magic to the Christmassy scene, as Rafe steered her through a busy throng of shoppers to where the taxi was waiting.

'Shall I take that?' He relieved her of Brand's gift and put it, along with the two small packages he was carrying, into the capacious pockets of his leather jacket.

As soon as they were settled in and underway, she found herself having to stifle a yawn. Wondering muzzily whether

her tiredness was due to champagne or jet lag, she fought against the urge to sleep.

But it was a slow journey back to Denver Court and when Rafe, seeing her eyelids start to droop, gathered her close, all she could feel was relief.

Comfortable, safe, at home, she let go and drifted into oblivion, her head on his shoulder.

When they reached their destination and drove into the forecourt she awakened naturally and, sitting up, looked around her.

There was a light covering of snow and it was still falling, whirling past like handfuls of thrown confetti, obliterating the tyre tracks of vehicles almost as soon as they were made.

She felt refreshed by the sleep. All the previous muzziness had vanished, and her head was clear.

'Feeling better now?' Rafe asked.

'Yes, I'm fine.'

'That's good. Later we're having dinner at the Starlight Room.'

When they had put on their coats and the bags and boxes had been retrieved, Rafe paid the driver, gave him a handsome tip and watched him sketch a salute as he drove away.

They crossed the foyer, with its Christmas tree and festive trimmings, and took the lift up to the penthouse. As it always had in the past, it made her nerves tighten and left her stomach behind.

When the doors slid open, juggling with the various packages, Rafe let them into his service flat and flicked on the lights.

With a little ache in her heart she realised that nothing had changed. It was the same as it had been when Rafe had brought her here more than a year ago, except that the patio and garden area now had a white coverlet.

Watching the snow falling softly, Madeleine found herself

thinking back to how pleasant it had been the summer she had known it, how they had drunk red wine and made love in the sun. How happy they had been.

Knowing that was a dangerous path to go down, she tried to push away the memory, but it crowded in, swamping her, overwhelming her.

Once again she could feel his beloved weight and the warmth of the sun on her face, smell his aftershave and the patio roses, taste the smooth dry wine on her tongue and the sweetness of his kisses…

'Penny for your thoughts.'

'What?'

As she turned away from the window, he said, 'You were miles away. Your face was soft and absorbed, and *waiting*, as though in your mind you were being made love to.'

Watching the hot colour pour into her cheeks, he said, 'It looks as though I hit the nail on the head. So who was it? Me?'

When she bit her lip and stayed silent, he shrugged. 'So long as it's turned you on, it doesn't really matter who it was.'

He carried the Harrod's packages through to the guest bedroom and dropped them onto a chaise longue covered in peach-coloured velvet, before helping her off with her coat.

At that moment the phone in the living room rang.

'If you'll excuse me, this might be the call I've been waiting for.' He went out, closing the door behind him.

Fiona? Madeleine wondered.

She was glad there wasn't a bedside phone. Had there been, she might have felt tempted to eavesdrop. But Rafe refused to have phones in the bedrooms on the grounds that, whether he was sleeping or making love, he didn't want to be disturbed.

Recalling what he'd said about having dinner at the Starlight Room, and realising she would need to get organised, she began to unpack the Harrod's parcels.

First of all the various toiletries, which she put into a toilet bag patterned with silvery-blue dolphins. Then, with a little quiver of excitement, she took out the evening dress Rafe had selected, and draped it over one of the button-backed chairs.

A simple ankle-length sheath with a modest neckline it was—on the surface—the kind of thing she might have chosen for herself. What made it totally different, apart from the designer label, was the superb cut, the colour and the material.

It was a clear, light gold—a colour she wouldn't normally have dreamt of buying—and it was made of silk chiffon.

As she had started to shake her head, the saleslady had said, 'It would look beautiful on, and madam certainly has the figure for it.'

'Try it,' Rafe had urged.

Soft and insubstantial as gossamer, it had slipped over her head and settled into place, a silken caress that clung lovingly to every curve.

The sight of herself in the full-length mirror had kept her momentarily rooted to the spot. She had never imagined she could look like this.

When, her knees feeling weak, she emerged from the fitting room, after one long look Rafe had said simply, 'Yes, we'll take it.'

As soon as a matching wrap and evening bag, strappy sandals and silk stockings had been purchased, he nodded his satisfaction. 'That's the most important part done. Now the lingerie department…'

The ivory silk undies, delicate as a spider's web, would have been any woman's dream, as would the dainty satin and lace nightdress and negligee he had picked out.

She had always bought pretty, feminine lingerie because it boosted her morale, but she had never aspired to anything in that class, and the thought of *wearing* such beautiful things had caused a shivery sensation to run up and down her spine.

Now looking down at them, she felt that same shiver of anticipation.

But she mustn't feel like this, she warned herself sharply. She mustn't allow herself to be lulled into meekly accepting what he wanted to give. She mustn't let herself enjoy the things he was almost forcing on her, perhaps just to salve his conscience.

If he had a conscience.

But after the way he had treated Fiona she couldn't believe he had.

Looking down at the ring on her finger, she wondered, not for the first time, how she could keep on loving a man like Rafe. A man who could treat one woman so badly, and coerce another into wearing his ring for 'the look of the thing' and for just as long as it suited him.

If he'd loved her it would have been different. Even if he hadn't intended to marry her it wouldn't have mattered. If he'd loved her, she could somehow have lived with that.

But he didn't love her. He might *want* her, but he didn't love her.

She must remember that and not weaken.

And if she stayed, she *would* weaken. So somehow she must find the will to leave him, and soon.

If she went back to Hethersage she would be trapped there, so it had to be tonight.

Judging by what he'd said in the taxi, he was confident that she would stay. So his guard would be down. With a bit of luck she could be in a cab and away before he missed her. Surely either Eve or Noel would be there to pay the fare. But if the worst came to the worst and they were both out, she would find some way of coping.

Feeling the need for action now she had made up her mind,

she decided to shower and start to get ready. Removing the ring and the small gold hoops from her ears, she put them on the bedside cabinet and took the pins from her hair. There was still no sign of Rafe as she gathered up the toilet bag and the negligee and headed for the *en suite* bathroom.

CHAPTER NINE

WHEN she emerged some fifteen minutes later, fresh and perfumed, the negligee whispering around her, her long hair a gleaming cloud around her shoulders, he was lounging on the chaise longue.

Stretching out a lazy hand, he pulled her down beside him in a proprietary manner, and nuzzled his face against the side of her neck. 'You smell delightful.'

Her heart starting to beat faster, she sat stiff and still, telling herself she mustn't weaken. If he was at all ruffled by her lack of response, he didn't show it.

Indicating the four small packages assembled by his side, he said, 'There's plenty of time to open your birthday presents before we need to get ready.'

Selecting the nearest, he handed it to her.

The gift was the one Carl Brand had given her and, stripping off the paper, she found a silver filigree case that opened to disclose a pale, padded lining with a dozen slots to hold rings. It was obviously an expensive item, and she realised that to give her something so valuable he must regard Rafe as an extremely good customer.

The second gift was a handmade card and a bottle of perfume from Katie. Absurdly touched that, as well as going to so much trouble over the card, the little girl had remembered that *Janvier* was her favourite perfume, Madeleine had to bite her lip.

Diane's gift was matching soap and bath oil.

'How did they know it was my birthday?'

'Apparently Katie once asked you when it was, and she'd remembered. That was one of the reasons she wanted to see you.' Rafe smiled at her. 'But when I told her I was planning to take you into town to buy your present, and that I had wanted it to be a surprise, she and Diane agreed not to say anything over lunch.'

He picked up the final package and, handing it to her, said, 'Happy birthday.'

The wrapping off, she saw it was the midnight-blue case with Marshall Brand in gold on the lid.

As, a tightness in her chest, she sat staring down at it, he asked, 'Aren't you going to open it?'

When her fingers, so sure at most times, fumbled ineffectually, he took it from her and used his thumbnail to flick open the lid.

Madeleine caught her breath involuntarily.

Lying on the velvet lining was a beautiful gold necklace set with six sparkling aquamarines. Alongside it were matching drop earrings that were equally lovely.

Watching her as she sat staring at the exquisite set in stunned silence, Rafe suggested crisply, 'Suppose you try them on?'

Her fingers far from steady, she fastened the earrings to her delicate lobes.

Head tilted a little to one side, he studied her. 'Perfect. Now for the necklace…'

As she made to pick it up, he said, 'No, let me.' Taking it from the case, he moved behind her and, having fastened it around her slender neck, bent to touch his lips to her nape.

She was still quivering from that caress when he turned her so that he could look at her.

'Yes… Though for the best effect they should be displayed against the skin.'

He brushed aside the ivory satin of the negligee.

The necklace felt smooth and cool against the warmth of her flesh, and through the dressing-table mirror she could see that the aquamarines were exactly the same colour as her eyes.

Remembering Rafe's comment, just for an instant she was overcome by emotion.

He saw that emotion and, misinterpreting it, said coldly, 'I suppose you're going to tell me that in spite of the ring, you feel like a kept woman.'

Angry that she'd weakened, she retorted, 'How else would you expect me to feel?'

He got up, his jaw tight. 'Well, if that's the case, I may as well have my money's worth.'

His hands beneath her elbows, he lifted her to her feet and, unfastening the belt of her negligee, slipped it from her shoulders. As it fell in a satin puddle at her feet he swept her up in his arms, carried her to the king-sized bed and laid her down.

Then quickly, but with no appearance of haste, he discarded his clothes and, like some sultan, stood looking down at her.

She was beautiful, with a slender body, long, balletic limbs and subtle curves.

But she was more than merely beautiful.

A great deal more.

That warm, generous mouth and those thickly lashed almond eyes made her a fascinating combination of wholesome girl-next-door and the exotic.

Her long blonde hair spreading over the pillow, and the blue-green aquamarines sparkling and glittering like a sunlit tropical sea against her creamy, flawless skin, added to that exoticism.

Slowly he ran a single finger from her throat to her navel, and back again.

Her heart thudding against her ribs, she stared up at him, her wide eyes fixed on his face.

Holding her gaze, he traced the curve of her breast and heard her breathing quicken as he circled the velvety nipple.

Knowing it would be useless, she made no attempt to fight him, but neither would she yield, she thought fiercely.

As though he could read her mood, he smiled a little grimly. When he moved to join her on the bed, she stiffened involuntarily. He might be aroused enough to just take her.

Perhaps, for one angry moment, he had intended to simply take, to impose his will, but it wasn't in his nature to force any woman.

Stretching out beside her, he touched his lips to hers in a slow, unhurried kiss, as though he was quite happy to spend the rest of the evening doing nothing else.

When her lips quivered and parted beneath his, he let his hands move over her, touching her as though she was some priceless treasure, more precious than the aquamarines she was wearing.

The caring, the tenderness, wrapped streamers of warmth around her heart and melted her resistance as easily as the heat from a candle flame melted wax.

His mouth followed his hands, leisurely, caressingly, finding the most sensitive areas. When he reached the soft skin of her inner thigh and began to flick with his tongue, she shuddered and made a little sound in her throat.

Softly, he murmured, 'Just lie there and enjoy what I'm going to do to you.'

Already on fire with need, she couldn't have done any other. He could feel her surrender to the sensations, surrender to him, as he teased and probed, building up the heat until pleasure exploded inside her and, her back arching, she clutched at the sheet she was lying on.

Still he didn't stop. Making the need build again and again.

Satisfying it again and again. Every time she knew there could be no more, there was more. When she finally felt his weight, she thought dazedly that she had nothing left to give, nothing left to gain.

But he proved her wrong.

Then common sense kicked in. Once again she had given in to him, allowed herself to be seduced, manipulated, when she should have been strong.

He might have *seemed* tender, caring, but it had merely been a show, and, while she couldn't deny how much pleasure he had given her, it had solved nothing. Altered nothing.

As though her thoughts had disturbed him, he stirred and lifted himself away. Then, sitting on the edge of the bed, he leaned over to kiss her lightly.

'It's about time we were moving.'

As she raised her hands, intending to take off the earrings and necklace, he stopped her. 'I want you to wear them…' Though he spoke softly, there was a steely edge to his tone.

He reached for the ring and, his expression precluding any argument, slipped it back on her finger. 'And your ring.'

Realising it was useless to argue, she agreed, 'Very well.'

She could get either Eve or Noel to return the jewellery and her unwanted finery to Rafe, and pick up her own things.

Watching him pad barefoot to the other bathroom, she thought, not for the first time, what a magnificent male animal he was. The lean hips and waist, the broad shoulders and elegant line of his spine, could have belonged to a Michelangelo statue. While his carriage, the way he held his head, spoke of a natural self-confidence, an innate authority.

Yet, if Diane was correct, he could so well have ended up weak and psychologically damaged. But while he appeared to be neither, he had no scruples about the way he treated women, Madeleine thought as she set about getting ready for the evening. But was that because, having been rejected by his mother, he was getting his own back on females in general?

That might explain his cruelty to Fiona.

But it didn't necessarily excuse it.

She had just finished putting the finishing touches to her make-up when Rafe reappeared wearing an immaculate dinner jacket, his seal-dark hair neatly brushed, his jaw freshly shaven.

Feeling, as always, the pull of his magnetism, she thought how devastatingly handsome he looked in evening clothes, and just how much she loved him.

Her breathing constricted, she wished she didn't have to leave him, wished that things could have been different, even while she knew how hopeless such a wish was.

Standing stock still, his head tilted a little to one side, he looked her over from head to toe, taking in the clinging dress with its matching gold sandals, the greeny-blue gems glittering at her ears and throat, the elegant knot of hair and the discreet touch of make-up.

Unnerved by the sheer intensity of his gaze, she asked awkwardly, 'Do I look all right?'

He smiled, the lopsided smile that never failed to touch her heart, and, lifting her hand to his lips, said huskily, 'My love, you look enchanting.'

Shaken to the core by the endearment, she was still standing motionless when he picked up her wrap and put it around her shoulders. 'As we won't be leaving the building, that's all you'll need.'

For what lay in store she could have done with a coat, but, unable to argue, she collected her small, gold evening bag and, on legs that felt unsteady, accompanied him out of the apartment.

As they went through an archway at the far end of the hallway and made their way along a series of marble galleries, she forced herself to think, to try and form a plan of escape.

Would it make sense to come back the same way? Or

would it be quicker to find another exit on the other side of the building?

As she was unsure where the exits were, or how easy it would be to get a taxi at any of them, it might be safer to stick with what she knew.

But it could take longer. Which would give Rafe a better chance of catching her up. For she was sure that when he missed her, he would come after her.

Though as soon as she was in a taxi and underway, she would be relatively safe. Of course, he would know only too well where she was heading, but once she got to Eve's she would be home and dry.

Then, somehow, she would put the last few days out of her mind and start to live the rest of her life. A life in which Rafe played no part.

She took a quick, ragged breath as the thought of never seeing him again cut into her heart like a knife. But it was the best way.

The only way.

Lifting her chin, she glanced up and found with a shock that his eyes were fixed on her face.

'Looking forward to the evening?' he asked, his voice casual.

'Oh, yes, enormously.' Wondering if she'd made the mistake of sounding too enthusiastic, she added, 'I've always dreamt of dancing and dining at the Starlight Room.'

'Then I'm delighted to have chosen the right venue,' he said smoothly.

The Starlight Room was, as its name suggested, a rooftop restaurant. It lay at the far end of the complex beyond a large skating rink, which in the summer became an open-air swimming pool.

Two storeys up and circular, an exotic mushroom on a thick stalk, the Starlight Room's projecting windows provided magnificent views over London.

Madeleine had seen it from a distance, but never yet been

inside, and as they stepped into the lift at the base she felt a little flutter of excitement.

As soon as they entered the luxurious foyer, a young man wearing immaculate evening dress wished them, 'Good evening, sir, madam,' and took Madeleine's wrap.

A moment later a larger-than-life *maître d'* appeared, who greeted Rafe by name, and with some ceremony led them through to the restaurant proper.

It was every bit as Arabian Nights and glamorous as she could have wished, with a table to each window and a central dance floor.

The majority of the tables were already occupied by a top-notch clientele wearing dinner jackets and evening gowns. The scent of French perfume hung on the air, and there were enough jewels on display to restock the Rue de la Paix.

It was the kind of gathering where ordinarily Madeleine might have felt out of her depth, even slightly intimidated by such a display of wealth. But with a little thrill of pride, she knew herself to be one of the best dressed women there. And on the arm of one of the most strikingly handsome, imposing men.

On a raised dais, like the hub of a wheel, a small orchestra was playing a Latin-American dance number, a soft, romantic tune, with a shiver of maracas.

Above them, the ceiling was a dome of indigo studded with lighted stars, and through the windows she could see snow was still falling gently, adding its own touch of magic to the scene.

Instead of a table for two, as she had imagined, they were shown to a table set for six. She glanced at Rafe, expecting him to point out the mistake, but he said nothing.

As soon as they had been seated, a waiter appeared with a magnum of champagne in an ice bucket and queried deferentially, 'Shall I open it, sir?'

'No, not yet, thanks.'

As the man moved away, Rafe turned to Madeleine, and asked, 'Shall we make the first part of your dream come true?'

Leaving her bag on the table, she went into his arms. He held her lightly but firmly, his spread hand at her waist steady, his chin just brushing the top of her head.

It was more than a year since they had danced together, and as they moved as one to the haunting rhythm she thought how happy she had been then.

Even now he'd contrived to make it lovely and romantic, and had things been different she could have danced the night away in his arms and been utterly content.

When the Latin-American medley came to an end with a scattering of applause, they started to make their way back to the table.

All at once, catching sight of who was sitting there, Madeleine's jaw dropped and she stopped dead in her tracks.

'Your mouth's open,' Rafe murmured in her ear, 'and it's giving me ideas I can't follow through in a public place.' He used a finger to lift her chin.

Then, an arm at her waist, he urged her towards the table, where, looking in their direction and smiling, were four people—Eve and Dave, Noel and, presumably, Zoe, all dressed up to the nines.

The four rose at their approach, and there was a smiling chorus of, 'Happy birthday,' before, gladness in her voice, Eve exclaimed, 'Just look at you!' and leaned forward to kiss Madeleine's cheek.

When Noel had followed suit, the three men shook hands with great cordiality.

How had Rafe and Noel come to be on such good terms? Madeleine wondered dazedly as, his glance moving from her to Rafe, Noel said with formal politeness, 'May I introduce Zoe Denholm…?

'Zoe, this is our lifelong friend, Madeleine Knight, and—' taking note of the aquamarine on Madeleine's finger '—her fiancé, Rafe Lombard.'

As they exchanged handshakes, Zoe said pleasantly, 'It's nice to meet you both.'

Looking at Madeleine's thunderstruck face, Eve turned to Rafe and remarked with satisfaction, 'It's quite obvious that you managed to keep the whole thing a secret.'

'It wasn't too hard.' Pulling out Madeleine's chair, he added with a wry smile, 'Her mind was on other things, wasn't it, sweetheart?'

When, still speechless, she sank onto it, he dropped a little kiss on the top of her head, a gesture that made Eve sigh sentimentally.

As the others resumed their seats, Zoe said to Madeleine, 'I've heard a great deal about you. I understand my darling idiot is hoping to bribe you to sing his praises.'

Seeing the fond, appreciative look she gave Noel, Madeleine found her voice and ventured, 'It doesn't appear to be necessary.'

'It isn't.'

As Noel began to preen himself, she gave him a dig in the ribs with her elbow. 'I know him much too well to be taken in.'

'I say, steady on there.' He looked aggrieved.

Smiling, she added, 'But I still love him,' and earned herself a squeeze.

'Let me see that.' Reaching across the table, Eve took Madeleine's hand and studied the ring. 'Wowee…and then some!

'I must confess that when Rafe and I first talked and he told me how things were and said he needed my help, I was a bit worried. But now, seeing how well it's all worked out, I couldn't be happier…'

What kind of lies had he told Eve to get both her and Noel so effortlessly on his side? Madeleine wondered numbly.

Fairly bubbling over with excitement, Eve added, 'And to put the gilt on the gingerbread, the Starlight Room! The mere idea of coming here to dine took my breath away.

'Though I'm afraid we won't be able to stay and dance. As soon as the meal's over we have to fly. We have first-row seats for *Serenade*, courtesy of Zoe, who is one of the co-writers.'

At a signal from Rafe, the waiter hurried over and, having opened the champagne with a satisfying pop, filled six flutes with the still-smoking wine.

After a toast to, 'The birthday girl,' they sipped champagne while they looked at the menu and ordered.

To Madeleine the whole thing seemed unreal, and, feeling as though she was caught up in some virtual-reality role-play, she chose at random.

When the waiter had gone, Eve and Noel each produced a nicely wrapped gift for her to open.

There was a bottle of her favourite hand and body lotion from Eve and Dave, and a luxurious box of chocolates from Noel and Zoe.

When she'd thanked them all, Dave, a nice-looking man with short brown hair and blue eyes, cleared his throat and glanced around. 'Without wishing to steal anyone's thunder, I've a question I've been going to ask Eve, and as tonight is somewhat special it seemed the right time to ask it.'

Taking her hand and holding it, he said simply, 'Will you marry me?'

'This madness much be catching,' Noel remarked into the momentary silence.

Clearly knocked off balance, Eve stammered, 'But I thought... I—I mean...I wasn't even sure you were happy living with me... Lately you've been so...so offhand.'

'Call it my last-ditch attempt to stay free. Like most males, I suppose, I was wary of committing myself, scared of being tied down.' He smiled quietly. 'But after that last row, I knew if I lost you I'd regret it for the rest of my life. So I went out and bought this…'

Fumbling in his pocket, he took out a small box and opened the lid. 'I'm afraid it won't look much against Madeleine's ring…'

'It's beautiful,' Eve said, her face all soft and glowing, and held out her hand so he could put the diamond twist onto her finger.

'Gosh, it even fits!' she exclaimed in wonder.

'So it should. I borrowed one of your dress rings to make sure I got the size right.'

'Darling.' She smiled mistily.

'Darling yourself.' He leaned towards her to kiss her on the lips.

There was a little burst of congratulations, then Rafe said, 'This calls for more champagne,' and refilled the glasses so they could drink a toast to the newly engaged pair.

On a high, the couples talked and laughed while they ate a superb meal, and if Rafe said little, and Madeleine even less, no one seemed to notice.

Then just as they were finishing coffee, a waiter appeared and murmured that their taxi was waiting.

In a moment, they had thanked their host and were on their feet and ready to leave. Stooping to give Madeleine a hug, Eve said, 'Ring me some time over the holiday and we'll have a good long talk.'

'Enjoy the show.' Rafe shook hands all round as they said their goodnights before hurrying off.

Sitting still as a statue, Madeleine watched them go and felt empty, as hollow inside as a ghost. Now it was too late she wondered if she'd done the right thing by keeping quiet.

Instead of letting them walk away believing everything was fine, should she have pricked the pretty bubble? Admitted how Rafe had treated her? Admitted just how fake her 'engagement' was?

If it had just been Eve and Noel, she might have done. Might have asked for their help. But as things were she couldn't have blurted it out in front of them all. Couldn't have blighted their evening.

Had Rafe been relying on that when he'd set up this birthday dinner?

Or, after the way she'd meekly got into his car at the Denaught, did he genuinely believe she wouldn't leave him?

If it was the latter, it showed a fair degree of arrogance on his part.

For a moment she wished she'd sent it all up in his face. But she couldn't have spoiled Dave's proposal and Eve's moment of glory, her radiant happiness…

'Would you like to dance?' Rafe asked, suddenly a polite stranger.

Squaring her shoulders, Madeleine shook her head. 'But I'd like to know what you told Eve to get her on your side.'

'The truth.'

'She already knew the truth.'

Rafe's green eyes flashed. 'She only knew what she'd heard from you, and that wasn't the truth.'

'If you think—'

He laid a finger on her lips. 'It's high time we set the score straight, but wc'll nccd to go back to thc flat and talk openly and honestly.'

'I'm not going back with you,' she said fiercely. If she went back with him she didn't trust herself not to weaken. 'I want to leave.'

'If you still want to leave when we've finished talking, I'll put you in a taxi and pay for a hotel for as long as you need one.

'But first, as it's your birthday, let's have one more dance.'

Rising to his feet, he held out his hand.

After a momentary hesitation, she put hers into it and let him lead her onto the dance floor.

The band were playing an old Jerome Kern tune, a slow foxtrot, dreamy and smoochy, and he held her close, his cheek against her hair.

But while part of her longed to give in to the magic, on-edge and needing to get to the bottom of Eve and Noel's volte-face, she could only be pleased when it was over.

As soon as he'd paid the bill and collected her wrap, they set off back to the flat.

It felt strange to be returning there when she had been so determined not to go back, and she wondered uneasily if she was doing the right thing.

Suppose this was just another trick to get her where he wanted her? He was good at tricks.

Her steps slowed and faltered. 'You promise that after we've talked you won't stop me leaving?'

He urged her forward. 'When you've heard me out, if you still want to leave, I promise I won't stop you.'

She sighed despairingly. What could he possibly say that would alter the situation enough to make her want to stay?

When they reached the flat, he suggested smoothly, 'While I put a match to the fire, why don't you change into something more comfortable?'

It suited her to get changed, and she went through to the bedroom without demure.

Her first act was to take off the ring, the necklace and the earrings, and place them safely in the case. That done, she put the beautiful dress and its accessories in the walk-in wardrobe, and donned the suit, boots and gold earrings she had worn earlier in the day.

If Rafe had been hoping she would change into her

negligee, she thought with a glimmer of humour, he was in for a big disappointment.

When she returned to the living room, a log fire was blazing cheerfully in the wide grate and two glasses, a bottle of brandy and a bottle of port with a paper napkin round the neck were waiting on a low table.

As she hesitated in the doorway, a gleam of irony in his green eyes, Rafe studied her suit and boots, but made no comment.

He'd taken off his jacket and black bow-tie, and the top two buttons of his evening shirt were undone, exposing the strong column of his throat. His sleeves were rolled up to his elbows, showing muscular arms lightly sprinkled with dark hair.

A smut adorned one cheek. As if her glance had made him conscious of it, he raised a hand to brush it away, and finished up with a smear. Without thinking, following her instincts, she reached for a napkin and touched her tongue to the corner to dampen it before wiping away the smear. Then, realising what she'd done, and annoyed with herself for doing it, she took a step backwards and, dropping the napkin onto the table as though it was red-hot, muttered, 'That was stupid.'

'No, it was sweet.' He took the hand that had held the napkin and raised it to his lips.

Flustered, looking anywhere but at him, she sat down in the nearest chair.

A second later, squatting in front of her, he began to remove her boots.

'I'll need them when I go,' she protested,

'*If* you go.'

Trying to regain ground, she insisted, '*When.*'

He shrugged. 'Have it your way, but if you keep them on in here you won't feel the good of them.'

For just a moment she softened at his care and attention, then, reminding herself she couldn't afford to, she frowned at him.

To her surprise he burst out laughing.

Without for a moment intending to, she found herself smiling back.

'That's better,' he applauded. Adding, 'Now then, port and brandy?'

'A small one, please.'

When he'd passed her a port and brandy and poured a brandy for himself, he took a seat opposite and, looking pointedly at her bare finger, said, 'You've taken off your ring.'

'Yes.' Then in a rush, 'I never wanted to wear it in the first place. I don't understand why you insisted on buying it.'

Lightly, he said, 'I believe in doing most things once, and I've never had the pleasure of buying an engagement ring before.'

'You bought Fiona a ring.' There—it was out.

'What makes you think that?'

When she hesitated, he said, 'I thought we were going to talk openly and honestly.'

After a moment, Madeleine admitted, 'She came to the clinic one night and asked to see me. She told me she was your fiancée. That you were engaged…'

'We were *never* engaged.' His answer was categoric.

'She was wearing a ring. A square-cut emerald.'

'Her grandmother gave her a square-cut emerald—a family heirloom, so to speak—for her twenty-first birthday. You can ask Harriet if you don't believe me.'

'Oh…'

'When Fiona told you she was my fiancée, what did you say?'

Remembrance of the hurt and humiliation she had suffered caused a spasm of pain to tighten Madeleine's face. 'I told her I had no idea you had a fiancée.'

'Was she a bitch to you?' he asked quietly.

'Not really. She said she didn't blame *me* in particular. That women threw themselves at you, so it was no wonder you took advantage, and if it hadn't been me it would have been some other woman.'

His green eyes narrowed. 'What else did she say?'

'That now she was home again it had to stop. You were hers. I remarked that if you were that kind of man I was surprised she still wanted you.

'She said, "Oh I want him all right, so if you were thinking of suggesting that I set him free, forget it… For one thing he doesn't want out, and for another, we have a bargain."'

'What kind of bargain?' Rafe asked curtly.

'She told me that her father, who didn't think a woman could successfully run a business, had been concerned about her future, and that he'd agreed to leave the whole of Charn Industries to you if you would marry her and take care of her. She added, "Rafe and I had been lovers for some time, so he was quite happy to make it legal."'

His green eyes glacial, he demanded, 'And you believed that'?

'Wasn't it the truth?'

He slammed his glass down on the table. 'No, it wasn't. Fiona and I were never lovers, and I never made any kind of bargain with my godfather.'

Though it was obvious he was quietly *furious*, she said steadily, 'But you inherited the Charn empire when he died.'

'Yes. Christopher had always intended to leave it to me. But after putting a considerable sum of money in trust for Fiona, he hit a rocky patch, and for the last few years of his life he was faced with severe financial problems.

'By the time he admitted the truth and asked me for help, his "empire" was teetering on the brink of collapse. It was only my financial support that kept it going…'

Was that what Diane had meant when she'd said, 'When Christopher ran into trouble, Rafe stood by him through thick and thin'?

'By the time he died,' Rafe went on flatly, 'I'd put so much capital into it that the whole kit and caboodle virtually belonged to me anyway.'

She had no doubt at all that he spoke the truth.

CHAPTER TEN

DEVASTATED by the realisation that she had been misjudging him all this time, she stared at him in stricken silence.

Seeing that devastation, Rafe bit back his anger and asked, 'Did Fiona say anything else?'

'That you and she would have been married by then and there wouldn't have been a problem if she hadn't been diagnosed with a rare blood disorder…'

'Go on,' Rafe urged.

The scene still engraved on her mind, Madeleine could clearly remember every word. 'She said, 'I've had to spend long periods in a private clinic, undergoing treatment, which meant Rafe was left alone, and as I say, he's a red-blooded man who needs a woman. Any woman… Then I discovered I was pregnant, which made this last treatment more prolonged and complicated, and in the end I lost the baby.'

A white line around his mouth, Rafe said grimly, 'And you believed that baby was mine?'

'W-well…y-yes,' she stammered. All the shock and distress she had felt evident in her voice, she went on, 'I was horrified to think that we'd been lovers while your fiancée went through such an ordeal…'

Sounding incredulous, he demanded, 'You really believed I could treat both her and you so shabbily?'

'I'm sorry…' The words tailed off at the fury on his face.

With a kind of raging calm, he said, 'Fiona was not my fiancée and the baby certainly wasn't mine. It couldn't *possibly* have been mine. There was never anything between us…'

Then what had made Fiona tell her such a tissue of lies? Madeleine wondered, but before she could ask, Rafe went on, 'Or perhaps I should say there was never anything on *my* part. I always thought of her, and treated her, as a much-loved sister.

'Unfortunately she developed a crush on me. I thought that when I went away to university it would die a natural death. But it didn't.

'When I made it clear that there could never be anything between us, that I just regarded her as a sister, she went completely off the rails and had relationships with several different men. Presumably one of them was the father…' He sighed in frustration.

'I'm sorry…sorry I blamed you…' Helplessly, she added, 'I didn't *want* to believe you could treat a sick woman in that way…'

Then, seeing the expression on his face, 'Or are you going to tell me she hadn't been ill, that that was a lie too?'

'The story about the blood disorder was a lie. But she had been ill…if you can call alcohol and drug dependency being ill. The clinics she was in and out of were alcohol- and drug-rehabilitation centres.' Madeleine gasped at his words.

Rafe went on, 'She got in with the wrong crowd, and before any of us realised she was hooked on drugs. It was an absolute nightmare. Each time she left some clinic and came home, we hoped and prayed she was cured. But each time she slipped back into her old ways. Then when her parents tried to get her to go in again for more treatment there'd be terrible scenes.

'For more than eighteen months Christopher was ill and frail, and even before he died Harriet couldn't cope, so it was up to me to take Fiona back and try to get her settled…'

So that was what Diane had meant when she said, 'The whole family were worried sick about her, though Rafe bore the brunt of it.'

'Do you remember the day I was supposed to pick you up to take you to see the Jonathan Cass pictures, and I couldn't make it?' he pursued.

'Yes, I remember. I'd been worried to death in case anything had happened to you. But you were in a strange mood. Though you must have known I wanted some kind of explanation, you wouldn't give me one.'

'*Couldn't*, rather than *wouldn't*.

'That morning I took Fiona back to the Tyler Rhodes Clinic and tried to get her settled in. At first she seemed calm enough, but after I told her I had to leave she became hysterical and violent.

'I couldn't just abandon her. I felt guilty and partly responsible. If I'd been able to love her in the way she wanted me to, things might have been different. Or if I hadn't gone to live with them in the first place...

'When I tried to call your flat to say I'd be late, she snatched the mobile out of my hand and threw it at the wall. Then after a bitter tirade she ran her nails down my face...'

So that was where the scratches had come from.

'It seems that somehow she'd found out about you, and was out of her mind with jealousy. I won't go into details, but that was one of the worst afternoons of my life.'

Feeling ashamed and sorry that she hadn't been more loving and supportive, Madeleine said, 'I wish you'd told me.'

'At the time I felt I couldn't. Though in retrospect I wish I had.'

'If only I'd known the truth I wouldn't have believed Fiona, wouldn't have presumed you'd just been using me and...' Remembering what had happened next, she broke off.

'Sent that email to get your own back?' he suggested bleakly.

'No, not to get my own back.'

His voice rough with anger and frustration, he asked, 'Why didn't you come to me? Why didn't you tell me what Fiona had said? Why, when I came to see what the hell was going on, did you stage that scene with Noel?'

'To save my pride,' she admitted.

'Despite the email, it came as a shock. I could hardly believe my eyes. It made me furiously angry and jealous... Even after Eve told me that you and Noel were like brother and sister, I was—'

'When did she tell you that?' Madeleine broke in.

'When I went to see her at the clinic.'

'What made you go?' Madeleine's voice was soft as she asked the one question that was really important.

'Because of a remark Fiona had made when Harriet mentioned you were coming home, she was convinced that it had been her daughter who was somehow responsible for our break-up. Remembering Noel, I could hardly believe it. But I decided to get to the bottom of things, so I rang Fiona and tackled her about it.

'Though she didn't tell me a fraction of what had been said, she admitted going to see you, admitted that she had claimed to be my fiancée. She said she was bitterly sorry, that she would have confessed sooner if she'd had the nerve.

'After talking to Fiona, I began to wonder about the rest, so I went to see Eve. I presumed she would know the score if anyone did... At first she was distinctly hostile, but when she heard the truth about Fiona things got easier.

'After I'd laid my cards on the table, she opened up and gave me all the information I needed. Including the fact that she was hoping to find a live-in position for you.

'When I told her that Harriet needed a live-in physiotherapist, and was staying with me at the hall, she agreed to help...'

Sighing, he admitted, 'But when I got you there, I didn't handle it very well. In fact that's the understatement of the year. I've been an absolute swine to you. I can't blame you for wanting to go, but I'm hoping you'll stay.'

Madeleine took a deep breath. 'There's something I'd like to ask you.'

'Ask away.'

'It's about Fiona. Diane said she was doing fine, that she'd been given a clean bill of health…'

'That right.'

'But I couldn't help but wonder where she was, what had happened to her…'

'A few weeks after she had been given that clean bill of health she married George Rampling's younger son, Mark, and they went to live in Edinburgh.

'A month ago their little boy was born. No two parents could have been happier, and Harriet and George were absolutely over the moon…'

Dazzled by the light, Madeleine said, 'So that's who they've gone up to Scotland to spend Christmas and New Year with.'

'That's right.'

Watching her face, Rafe asked, 'Does knowing that make it any easier for you to stay? At least for tonight.'

'If I do stay—'

'It will be on your terms,' he broke in quickly. 'I promise I won't try to bulldoze you in any way, and it will give you a chance to think things over. What do you say?'

'Very well,' she said and saw the flicker of relief he couldn't hide.

Getting to her feet, she stifled a yawn. 'I'd like to go to bed.'

'Alone?' he queried.

'Alone.'

Rising, he lifted her hand to his lips. 'Then I'll say goodnight.'

'Goodnight.' She picked up her boots and went.

Rafe had suggested that staying over would provide a chance to think, but, as though both her brain and body had shut down, she felt completely drained and weary, too tired to think.

She changed into her night things like some zombie, and slept as soon as her head touched the pillow.

When she surfaced the next morning, the clock said almost ten-thirty. It was, she realised, Christmas Eve, and decision time.

Before she could begin to think, however, there was a tap at the door, and a second later Rafe's voice queried, 'Ready for some toast and coffee?'

Her heart gave a little leap. Thinking how careful he was being, how circumspect, as though it *mattered* to him, she sat up and answered, 'Please.'

He offloaded a pot of coffee and a jug of warm milk before settling the tray across her knees.

On it, as well as toast, butter and marmalade, was a glass of freshly squeezed orange juice and a perfect hothouse rosebud, its dark red, velvety petals gloriously scented.

The fact that he'd gone to so much trouble touched her heart.

'I was planning to have lunch at the Denaught and fly back to Hethersage Hall this afternoon,' he told her. 'Will you come and spend Christmas there? Simply as a guest.'

When she didn't immediately answer, he suggested, 'Give it some thought while you eat your breakfast.' He turned away, and a moment later the door had closed quietly behind him.

She fought down an urge to call him back.

Having decided he'd made a mistake by bulldozing her, he was being cautious, giving her time, breathing space. She should value that, rather than doing anything impulsive.

While she buttered and ate a slice of toast and drank a cup of coffee, she tried to follow Rafe's suggestion and think.

Though she bitterly regretted not trusting him and ruining

what they might have had, common sense told her that it was no use repining. Nothing could be altered. All she could do was put the past behind her and move forward.

So was she prepared to stay and give him what he wanted? While she loved him, could she cope with knowing he didn't love her?

But she didn't have to make up her mind about that straight away. Spending Christmas at the hall would give her time to think, to decide.

Setting the tray aside, she got out of bed and showered and dressed in record time. Then, putting the rose, the stem of which she'd wrapped in dampened cotton-wool wipes, into her shoulder-bag, she picked up her coat and the case with its precious jewellery, and went through to the living room.

Rafe was standing by the French windows with his back to the room, staring out over the snowy patio. His whole body looked taut, and she could see the tension in his neck and shoulders.

When he turned round slowly and looked at her, she went over to him and handed him the jewel case.

'Does that mean you've decided not to come?'

'No...I...I haven't really decided.'

She saw the flare of hope, before a shutter came down and he asked levelly, 'So the question is, yes or no?'

'You said simply as a guest?'

His eyes on her face, he agreed, 'Yes.'

'Then I'll come.'

His little sigh was audible. 'In that case I'll ask them to bring the car round, and let Jack know roughly what time we'll be back.'

Though there was bright sunshine and a sky of clear, Mediterranean blue, it was a bitterly cold day with a fresh covering of sparkling snow.

Apart from Rafe remarking that it was good flying weather, the drive to the Denaught was accomplished in silence.

After a brief discussion of the menu, and some recommendations on Rafe's part, lunch too was a silent meal.

But where in the past their silences had been comfortable, companionable, now there was a tension between them that stretched like fine wire. Wire that Madeleine wanted to snap.

But she could think of nothing to say.

She was relieved when lunch was over and they were installed in the helicopter and underway. A lot less nervous this time, she would have enjoyed the flight if she hadn't been worrying about the coming hours and days.

In the west the sun had gone down in a blaze of pink and gold, and a blue dusk was just starting to gather as they descended towards the cleared helicopter pad.

Wearing what appeared to be thigh-length rubber boots, Jack was just emerging from the hangar with a gleaming two-seater snowmobile.

When the rotor blades had almost stopped turning Rafe removed his headset and, jumping out, came round to help her out.

'I've a few things to take care of, so Jack will run you back to the house.'

As soon as Madeleine was installed on the passenger seat, Jack handed her a blue helmet. 'If you'd like to put this on, miss… It isn't far, as you know, but I always say, you can't be too careful.'

She thanked him and buckled the strap into place.

When they reached the house the door was opened by a young, round-faced woman with pale blue eyes and sandy hair, who ushered her inside.

'Miss Knight…I'm Annie… I've lit a fire in your flat and left fresh bread and milk in the kitchen. If there's anything else you need, you only have to ask.

'Dinner's at seven-thirty. In the meantime, if you'd like me to bring a nice pot of tea to the living room…?'

'Thank you, Annie, but I think I'll go straight up to the flat.'

As she crossed the hall and made her way upstairs, she felt an odd sense of coming home, as if the old house recognised her presence and welcomed her back.

There was a bright fire burning in the living-room grate, and when Madeleine had put the rose in water and made herself a pot of tea, instead of switching on the light she sat down in the fireglow.

Had she done the right thing in coming back to Hethersage Hall? she wondered. Or should she have been stronger and walked away?

But it was useless to hark back, and too soon to try and think ahead. She would just let go for the present and drift.

The comfort and warmth were soporific, and in spite of her good night's sleep her eyelids gradually closed…

When she awoke, the fire was dying into whitish ash and it was dark apart from a mere glimmer of snowy light coming through the window.

She was just wondering how long she'd slept when the clock on the mantel chimed six-thirty. Time she was getting ready to go down to dinner.

Switching on the light, she went through to the bedroom to shower and change into a midnight-blue sheath, before re-coiling her hair and putting on fresh make-up.

Despite her attempts to stay calm, butterflies were dancing in her stomach as she made her way down to the study and opened the door.

The cosy room was lit by a single standard lamp, and for an instant she thought it was empty. Then she saw Rafe was already there, leaning against the mantel, flickering firelight turning his lean face into a changing mask of bronze and black.

She had the impression that he'd been standing there some time, staring blindly into space.

He glanced up as she came in, and for an instant his face looked taut and tired before a shutter came down and, assuming the role of polite host, he came forward to greet her.

While they had a pre-dinner drink he made polite conversation, and though her heart ached that, having been so close, they should come to this, she followed his lead as best she could.

Though they both tried their hardest, dinner was another uncomfortable meal, and by the time they returned to the study for a nightcap in front of the fire, Madeleine was regretting coming and wondering how soon she could escape to bed.

The curtains hadn't been pulled across the windows and through the diamond-leaded panes she could see that snow was falling.

Into the silence, she remarked, 'It's some time since we had a white Christmas.'

Rafe glanced up from pouring brandy into two goblets. 'The Met Office forecast it.'

'Yes. Noel said so when I was still in Boston.'

'What made you decide to come back to England?'

'When I heard Eve's voice I knew I was homesick.'

'You asked her opinion on whether or not you should marry Alan.' It was a statement not a question.

Madeleine sighed. 'Eve's wise. She said the mere fact that I *had* to ask her opinion proved I didn't love him enough. And of course she was quite right.'

Rafe's eyes met and held hers, as he said quietly, 'I had hoped at one time that you might love me…'

Feeling as though her chest was being constricted, she admitted, 'I did.'

It was his turn to sigh. 'If I'd asked you to marry me then, would you have done?'

She hesitated, before saying in a rush, 'Yes, if I'd been sure you loved me.'

'Oh, yes, I loved you. The instant I saw your face, it was like being socked on the jaw. Rocked back on my heels, I tried to tell myself that what I felt might just be lust, but even then I knew it was love.

'I didn't know you, didn't know what went on inside your head, how your mind worked, what made you happy, what made you sad. I didn't know you had a sense of humour, or that you liked children. I didn't know you had courage and compassion, and not a nasty bone in your body. All I knew was that you were the woman I'd been waiting for. The woman I wanted to marry. I had planned to propose to you in Paris, to take you to the Rue de la Paix to choose a ring...'

Her heart seemed to turn over in her breast.

'That's why I was so devastated when I saw you with Noel. I didn't want to believe it. I might not have, if I hadn't known that all through our relationship you'd been hiding something.'

When she made no attempt to deny it, he went on, 'Every unexplained absence made me wonder if you were seeing another man. Were you?'

'No.'

'Then why all the secrecy? Why wouldn't you tell me where you went?' His frustration evident, he added, 'I still don't know.'

'I went to the Pastures Nursing Home to see my mother,' Madeleine blurted out. 'She'd been in a coma for more than a year. She was injured in the same gas explosion that killed Colin.'

He looked up sharply. 'Why didn't you tell me?'

Her voice unsteady, she admitted, 'Because I felt so guilty...'

'Guilty?'

'Guilty that she was there… Guilty that Colin had died… Guilty that I hadn't really loved him…' Her eyes filled with tears.

Rafe reached out and took her hand. 'Tell me,' he said quietly. 'Start at the beginning and tell me everything.'

When she had herself under control, she began tonelessly, 'Colin was a very nice-looking man and a well-respected tutor. When he first took an interest in me I was flattered.

'I enjoyed his company and what I saw then as his maturity, and, imagining myself in love, I agreed to marry him. Perhaps I was looking for a father figure, I don't know…

'As soon as I got my degree, we were married at a register office. He'd been sharing a small flat with a male colleague, so we moved in with my mother while we looked for a place of our own. Mum and he got on well together, and we were still there when the accident happened…'

'You weren't involved?'

Madeleine shook her head. 'No. I was out shopping.'

'Go on.'

'We'd only been married a short time when I realised I'd made a terrible mistake. I started to feel trapped, and that made me on-edge. We began to have minor quarrels, tiffs over things that didn't really matter.'

Her voice wobbled a little, and Rafe gave her hand a squeeze.

After a moment, she went on, 'On Saturdays, when Mum and I did the week's grocery shopping, Colin used to come with us…'

Rafe raised an eyebrow. 'Most men detest that kind of shopping.'

'He'd been a bachelor for a long time and he'd grown fussy about what he ate… Afterwards we'd all have lunch together at Bennets—the only place Colin would go to.'

'Go on.'

'The explosion happened just before lunch time on a Saturday. If we'd followed our usual routine we would have all been out. But at breakfast that morning, when Colin complained about the marmalade I snapped at him, and we ended up quarrelling yet again.

'I wanted some breathing space, and that must have been obvious to Mum, because she suggested that I went shopping alone while Colin helped her finish the living room she'd been redecorating.

'A new hearth had just been put in, and they discovered afterwards that a gas pipe leading to the log-effect fire had been fractured, which must have caused a build-up of gas behind the tiling. Colin was putting up bookshelves next to the fireplace... Using an electric drill...

'I got back to find the house had been wrecked and Mum and Colin had been taken to hospital. Colin was dead when I got there.'

Rafe saw the numbness of despair on her face.

'So all this time you've been blaming yourself.'

'I was to blame.'

'Don't be foolish,' he said gently. 'It was an accident waiting to happen. If the three of you had gone shopping and had lunch out as usual, it would still have happened sooner or later...'

His rational explanation seemed to help clear her mind, and made her see the scenario differently. For some reason the inevitability of the accident had never occurred to her.

Rafe went on, 'And, when it's too late, a lot of people must discover they've made a mistake and married the wrong person. It's not something to blame yourself for.'

As she felt the weight of guilt easing, he asked, 'What about your mother?'

'She died a few days after we split up.'

'Dear God,' he muttered.

'If she'd still been alive I would never have gone to the States. As it was, I felt I had nothing left. I wanted to get away, to put all the pain and sadness behind me. I soon discovered it wasn't possible…'

'No.'

There was a long silence, before Rafe continued, 'When you went I told myself I was glad. The further away the better. But I found I couldn't let go. I had to know what you were doing, how you were. When I learnt you were coming home, it was with mixed emotions. Then after I'd talked to Eve and discovered that the whole charade had been in response to Fiona's lies, that it had been she and Noel who had suggested the "other man" scenario, at first all I could feel was relief—'

'There's something I don't understand,' Madeleine broke in. 'If you already knew the truth about Noel and me, why were you so horrible to me? Why did you talk about reparation?'

'After the first flood of relief, anger kicked in. I was furious with you for not telling me about Fiona, furious with you for believing her lies, for not trusting me…

'I just went mad. I blamed your lack of trust for all the pain and anguish, for losing us more than a year of our lives…'

If only that were all that had been lost.

'Now the only thing I can do is apologise for the way I treated you…'

If only she *had* trusted him, instead of just becoming an obsession, something he wanted to free himself from, she might have kept his love.

Her eyes sparkled like jewels as tears welled up and splashed down her cheeks.

He rose as if to comfort her, then, as though he'd had second thoughts, he sat down again and passed her a spotless handkerchief.

'Thank you,' she mumbled. She had just finished mopping her face and blowing her nose when she heard the strains of *O, Little Town of Bethlehem.*

Glancing at the window, she saw that a group of perhaps

twelve people had collected. They were muffled up in scarves and gloves and woolly hats, and carrying carol sheets and candle-lanterns.

Turning startled eyes on Rafe, she saw he looked anything but surprised.

'You were expecting them.'

'Yes.'

'Who are they?'

'Estate staff. Most of them worked for the previous owner, and apparently it's become the custom for them to gather on Christmas Eve to sing carols.

'Then they assemble in the hall for dinner and a glass or two of mulled wine, which hopefully Annie will have waiting.'

Taking Madeleine's hand, he drew her over to the window, and they stood hand in hand, listening, while the small company sang their way through all the old familiar carols.

As *We Wish You a Merry Christmas and a Happy New Year* came to an end, the group dispersed.

'Come on,' Rafe said, taking Madeleine's hand and leading her into the hall, where a huge log fire was blazing.

They got to the door just as the knock came. Throwing it open, he welcomed the singers inside.

As they all trooped in, stamping snow off their boots and wellingtons, Annie wheeled in a trolley loaded with a punch bowl full of steaming wine and glass cups with handles. Several plates were piled high with hot mince pies and other festive fare.

'Thank you, Annie.' Taking a long-handled ladle, Rafe filled the cups himself and handed them out, amidst much cheerful talk and laughter.

Rather than just stand there, Madeleine picked up a plate and began to hand round the food.

Catching her eye, Rafe smiled at her.

As she smiled back it crossed her mind that they could have been master and mistress of the hall, following the traditions of the season while their children slept upstairs dreaming of sleigh bells and Santa Claus.

The thought made a lump come into her throat.

By the time everyone had eaten and drunk their fill it was almost a quarter to twelve.

'Well, I'd best be getting back,' one man said. 'I've got to dress up and play Father Christmas for the youngsters.'

'Why dress up?' another asked. 'Surely they'll be fast asleep?'

'Can't take any chances,' the first one replied. 'Last year they spent most of the night wide awake.'

'Well, I don't have to worry. My twins are only eight months old, and both good sleepers.'

'You just wait…'

On that note, with many thanks, and calls of, 'A merry Christmas,' they headed for the door and suddenly Rafe and Madeleine were alone.

'Shall we go back to the living room?' he asked.

Still trying to swallow past the lump in her throat, and tired, despite her earlier sleep, she shook her head. 'It's getting quite late; I think I'll go to bed.'

He nodded in agreement. 'I'll see you up.'

They climbed the stairs in silence.

When they reached the door of her flat she paused, hoping he would take her in his arms, kiss her, ask to stay, do *something*…

'Goodnight.' He raised her hand to his lips, and turned away.

Flattened, she let him go and went inside to get ready for bed.

A glance at the clock showed it was already Christmas Day, but somehow she no longer felt tired, and even when she was tucked up warm and comfortable sleep evaded her.

All she could think was, had Rafe done as she'd hoped, they would be together now.

But, having apologised for the way he had treated her, he

seemed determined to stand back and let her decide the next move.

She wanted to stay. She knew that now. Admitted it. Even though a happy ending was unlikely, she wanted to be with him for as long as possible.

But how could she stay knowing Rafe had loved her and she had killed that love? Her pride balked at staying with a man who merely wanted to use her.

So at the end of the holiday were she and her pride going to walk away hand in hand?

Didn't she owe it to herself?

But it had been *her* stupidity that had caused them both so much pain and anguish.

Rafe had been blameless.

Didn't she owe *him* something?

There was no way she could alter the past, and she might not be able to make up for everything, but she could make *some* reparation.

She got out of bed and, taking off her nightdress replaced it with a robe before going quietly out of the flat and along the dark passage to Rafe's door.

Without knocking she slipped silently into his room, feeling first the smooth floorboards and then the soft brush of a rug beneath her bare feet.

In the snowy light that came through the open curtains she could make out the polished wood of the four-poster and his dark head on the pillow.

She unbelted her robe and let it drop at her feet, then, lifting the duvet, slid into bed beside him.

He slept naked. His breathing was soft and even, his eyes were closed and she could see the fan of dark lashes lying on his hard cheeks.

Supporting herself on one elbow, she leaned to kiss his

lips and saw the gleam of his eyes a moment before his arms went round her.

His voice husky, he asked, 'Do I take it this is my Christmas present?'

'Are you happy with it?'

'It has to be the best I ever had. I hope what I'm giving you comes up to it.'

'What are you giving me?'

Reaching out a long arm, he switched on the bedside light and passed her a small gift-wrapped package. 'Take a look.'

Inside was the bracelet she had admired in Marshall Brand, and with it a chased-gold wedding ring that matched the engagement ring he'd bought.

'Marry me,' he said simply.

'B-but you said I was just an obsession…that you needed to get me out of your system…'

'When I told Eve that I'd never stopped loving you and I wanted you back, she said she was sure you still loved me. It was only when I began to think she was mistaken that I panicked and did and said all kinds of stupid things. *Do* you still love me?'

'Yes,' she said. There would be plenty of time in the coming years to tell him just how much.

'Then answer my question, woman.'

'Well, I might need persuading…'

The words ended in a startled squeak as he rolled, pinning her beneath him. 'How much persuading?'

'Quite a lot,' she said demurely. 'So I hope you're up to it.'

'You can count on me. We'll start with a kiss, shall we, and progress from there?'

'A good start,' she murmured, when he'd kissed her deeply. 'What comes next?'

'This.' He proceeded to demonstrate.

Caught up in the magic he wove so well, she was soon wrapped in black velvet, yet full of heat and light. Glowing. Burning. Incandescent.

His lovemaking culminated in a fire-storm of sensation so intense that she couldn't breathe, couldn't think, couldn't see.

When the fierce sexual heat was replaced by the warmth of belonging and she lay quietly in his arms, he asked, 'How was that?'

'Wonderful,' she murmured. 'You've just upped your chances of a yes vote.'

'I'm glad to be getting somewhere. Of course, to do a *thorough* job of persuading will take some considerable time, but no one can blame us if we spend Christmas Day in bed.'

'No, indeed,' she agreed happily.

MILLS & BOON®

Live the emotion

Modern
romance™

THE SECRET BABY REVENGE by *Emma Darcy*

Joaquin Luis Sola yearns to possess beautiful Nicole
Ashton, who left him five years ago. Now Nicole is willing
to offer herself to him, if he will pay her debts. This
proposition promises that he will see a most satisfying
return...

THE PRINCE'S VIRGIN WIFE by *Lucy Monroe*

Principe Tomasso Scorsolini's late consort was a terrible
mother. Now Tomasso wants a *suitable* bride... Maggie
can't believe that the Prince has chosen her – but
she soon realises Tomasso wants only a marriage of
convenience, not a wife he will love...

TAKEN FOR HIS PLEASURE by *Carol Marinelli*

When detective Lydia Holmes is assigned to pose as
a mistress to rebel billionaire Anton Santini, she finds
it hard to maintain her professional façade around the
sexy Italian. Anton takes her to his bedroom... For his
pleasure... But doesn't expect what she gives in return...

AT THE GREEK TYCOON'S BIDDING
by *Cathy Williams*

Heather is different from Greek businessman Theo
Miquel's usual prey: frumpy, far too talkative and his office
cleaner. But Theo could see she would be perfect for
an affair. At his beck and call until he tires of her... But
Heather won't stay at her boss's bidding!

On sale 7th July 2006

*Available at WHSmith, Tesco, ASDA, Borders, Eason,
Sainsbury's and most bookshops*

www.millsandboon.co.uk

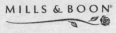

MILLS & BOON®

Live the emotion

In July 2006 Mills & Boon bring back
two of their classic collections, each
featuring three favourite romances by
our bestselling authors…

Marrying
the
Millionaire

by Lynne Graham
Featuring
An Arabian Marriage
The Disobedient Mistress
The Heiress Bride

**Make sure you buy these
irresistible stories!**

On sale 7th July 2006

*Available at WHSmith, Tesco, ASDA, Borders, Eason,
Sainsbury's and most bookshops*

www.millsandboon.co.uk

Look for these exciting new titles on Mills & Boon Audio CDs on sale from 5th May 2006

The Greek's Chosen Wife by Lynne Graham
Wife Against Her Will by Sara Craven

A Practical Mistress by Mary Brendan
The Gladiator's Honour by Michelle Styles

MILLS & BOON®

www.millsandboon.co.uk

FREE!

4 Books

and a surprise gift!

We would like to take this opportunity to thank you for reading this Mills & Boon® book by offering you the chance to take FOUR more specially selected titles from the Modern Romance™ series absolutely FREE! We're also making this offer to introduce you to the benefits of the Reader Service™—

- ★ **FREE home delivery**
- ★ **FREE gifts and competitions**
- ★ **FREE monthly Newsletter**
- ★ **Exclusive Reader Service offers**
- ★ **Books available before they're in the shops**

Accepting these FREE books and gift places you under no obligation to buy, you may cancel at any time, even after receiving your free shipment. Simply complete your details below and return the entire page to the address below. You don't even need a stamp!

YES! Please send me 4 free Modern Romance books and a surprise gift. I understand that unless you hear from me, I will receive 6 superb new titles every month for just £2.80 each, postage and packing free. I am under no obligation to purchase any books and may cancel my subscription at any time. The free books and gift will be mine to keep in any case.

P6ZEF

Ms/Mrs/Miss/Mr ....Initials ....

BLOCK CAPITALS PLEASE

Surname ....

Address ....

....

....Postcode ....

Send this whole page to:
UK: FREEPOST CN81, Croydon, CR9 3WZ

Offer valid in UK only and is not available to current Reader service subscribers to this series. Overseas and Eire please write for details. We reserve the right to refuse an application and applicants must be aged 18 years or over. Only one application per household. Terms and prices subject to change without notice. Offer expires 30th September 2006. As a result of this application, you may receive offers from Harlequin Mills & Boon and other carefully selected companies. If you would prefer not to share in this opportunity please write to The Data Manager, PO Box 676, Richmond, TW9 1WU.

Mills & Boon® is a registered trademark owned by Harlequin Mills & Boon Limited.
Modern Romance™ is being used as a trademark. The Reader Service™ is being used as a trademark.